Robert F. Murphy, Yolanda Murphy

Shoshone-Bannock Subsistence and Society

e-artnow 2024

Robert F. Murphy, Yolanda Murphy

Shoshone-Bannock Subsistence and Society

e-artnow, 2024
Contact: eartnow.info@gmail.com

ISBN: 978-80-273-8906-3

Contents

PREFACE

During the years 1954 to 1957, the authors engaged in ethnographic and historic research on the Shoshone and Bannock Indians under the sponsorship of the Lands Division of the Department of Justice in connection with one of a number of suits brought by Indian tribes for compensation for territory lost to the advancing frontier. The action was brought jointly by the Shoshone Indians of Wyoming, Idaho, Utah, and Nevada, and the Bannock of Idaho; it excluded the Shoshonean speakers of California, and the Bannock remained separate from the suit brought by their colinguists, the Northern Paiute of Oregon and Idaho.

Most anthropologists are aware of the ethnographic issues involved in the Indian lands claims cases, for the profession has had an active role in them. Of central importance, of course, is the question of the extent of territory used and occupied by the tribe in litigation. Other basic problems include the determination of the nature and composition of the groups involved, the rhythm of their seasonal activity, their political identity, and the actual time at which they occupied and used the terrain. Beyond these specifically anthropological considerations, other professionals have had an equally important role in delivering expert testimony in the cases, and we wish only to note in passing that historians, land appraisers, attorneys, and others have had much to do with their outcome.

The extent of the territory in question and the complexity of the historical period in point, that preceding the treaties of 1863 and 1868, required considerable research. We spent the summer of 1954 on the Shoshone reservations at Wind River, Wyoming, Fort Hall, Idaho, and Duck Valley, Nevada. Some six weeks each were spent at Wind River and Fort Hall and a week at Duck Valley. At each of these places we spoke to the oldest informants available. Salvage ethnography of this type is generally an unrewarding and unsatisfying task, and it was complicated in this investigation by the fact that we were asking our informants to recall historical material that is often ill preserved in the oral tradition. Thus, an old Indian may well remember some custom connected with war or ceremony that he had either experienced or that had been told to him by an older person. But he would be less likely to recall the exact places where game could be found, the trails used, the organization and composition of the group that pursued the game, and so forth. This is especially true of the buffalo-hunting Shoshone, for any informant who actually took part in a hunt as a mature individual would have been in his late seventies, at least, at the time of our research. And informants did not, of course, distinguish clearly between pre-and post-reservation times. Only careful cross-checking would reveal whether the individual was speaking of the 1860's or the 1890's. As might be expected, it was virtually impossible to determine whether the data supposedly valid for the 1860's was true of the preceding decade or the one before that, and any student of Plains and Basin-Plateau history recognizes that such historical continuity cannot be assumed.

Because of these limitations on the reliability of informants, most of our work was by necessity based on ethnohistoric research. Every attempt was made to examine the most important literature on the area and period. The total number of sources scrutinized far exceeded the bibliography at the end of this monograph, for many of them contained data that were at best scanty and superficial and at worst totally false. Despite our best efforts to approximate an adequate historical criticism, some of the data presented were found in works that can be used only with great caution. Alexander Ross, for example, has reported much material of doubtful authenticity, and one may labor long and hard in the accounts of Jim Beckwourth to separate fact from a delightful tendency to make the story exciting and his own personage more impressive. It is a wry commentary on the veracity of the mountain men that John Coulter's account of Yellowstone Park was long laughed at by his own peers as being simply an addition to a snowballing folklore of the fur country. Among other dubious sources, we can add W. T. Hamilton and the Irving account of Captain Bonneville's adventures. The problem of criticism becomes particularly difficult during the fur period from about 1810 to 1840 owing to the paucity of sources available for cross-checking particular data. Bonneville and Ross are especially rich in information, most of which cannot be easily verified. The choice became one of dismissing them altogether or using them. We elected to use them, but we have attempted restraint in drawing any important conclusions from them.

The monograph follows substantially the report submitted to the Indian Claims Commission. It has been edited, and we have also shifted emphasis at certain points to our own special interests. These are concerned with the relations between the social groups of the Basin and those of the Plains and the impact of the ecology of either region upon the social structures of the native population. A few qualifications should be noted. The limitations imposed by our assignment and by time did not allow the collection of as full a range of material on social structure as would be wished. Also, we have excluded any discussion of the Shoshone of Nevada, for our field work there was far too brief. Our one week at Duck Valley only served to reinforce our opinion of the truly masterful ethnography represented by Steward's "Basin-Plateau Aboriginal Sociopolitical Groups," and we could add little to his work.

Finally, we wish to acknowledge our indebtedness to the Board of Editors of the University of California Publications in Anthropological Records for their valuable comments and to our many friends on the reservations visited for their friendship and coöperation. We have also profited greatly from discussions with Drs. Sven Liljeblad, Åke Hultkranz, and Julian Steward. This work owes much of whatever merit it may be found to have, and none of its shortcomings, to all these people.

Robert F. Murphy

Yolanda Murphy

I. THE NORTHERN AND EASTERN SHOSHONE

The Rocky Mountain range was not an insuperable obstacle to communication between the Indian tribes east and west of the Continental Divide. The Arapaho, Cheyenne, Crow, Blackfoot, and other peoples of the Plains often crossed the range for purposes of hunting, warfare, and trade. And the tribes of the Basin-Plateau region also traversed the spine of the continent with much the same ends in mind. But their needs were more urgent, for in the late historic period the western part of the Great Plains of North America constituted the last reserve of the bison, the game staple of the Indian population of the western slope of the Rockies. Thus was established the pattern of transmontane buffalo hunting, first reported by Lewis and Clark and studied latterly by many anthropologists. The present volume represents a further contribution to this research.

The Rocky Mountains are traversible by horse in all sections. In Montana, the passes are only 5,000 to 7,000 feet in elevation, and the Indians crossed over the same routes followed today by highways. The Wyoming Rockies similarly presented no serious problem to nomadic peoples. Although the Yellowstone Park area posed some difficulty for travel, a more southerly route led over South Pass at a gentle gradient only 7,550 feet in altitude. That the mountains were no great challenge is illustrated by the fact that Indians traveling from Green River to Wind River often preferred to take more direct routes through passes over 10,000 feet high rather than to follow the more circuitous trail over South Pass. Farther south, the Colorado Rockies and their passes are far more lofty, but even these high ranges did not totally prevent travel. None of these areas, of course, could be traversed in the winter. When the snow left the high country in late spring and early summer, however, the mountains were not only avenues of travel, but they were also hunting grounds. None of the buffalo hunters relied completely on that animal for food, and the high mountain parks abounded in elk, bighorn sheep, moose, and deer. Streams were fished, berries were gathered along their banks, and roots were dug in the surrounding hills. For the tribes living on their flanks, the mountains afforded an important source of subsistence.

If the Rocky Mountains did not effectively isolate Plains societies from those of the Basin-Plateau, differences in environment certainly did. Plains economy was based upon two animals, the horse and the buffalo, both of which depended on sufficient grass for forage. The horse diffused northward along both sides of the mountains, and the richest herds were probably found among the Plateau tribes and not in the Plains (cf. Ewers, 1955, p. 28). The greatest herds of buffalo were found east of the Continental Divide, however, although smaller and more scattered herds roamed the regions of higher elevation and rainfall, immediately west of the Rockies, until about 1840. Thus, although the standard image of "Plains culture" is derived from the short-grass country east of the Divide, the tribes living west of the mountains were also mounted and also had access to buffalo. Their varying involvement in this subsistence pursuit and its associated technology, combined with the diffusion of other items of culture, resulted in what Kroeber has called "a late Plains overlay" of culture in the area (Kroeber, 1939, p. 52).

The spread of Plains culture into the Basin-Plateau area has been described by Wissler, Lowie, and others, the emphasis usually being upon traits of material culture. Less research has been devoted to the impact of equestrian life and the pursuit of the buffalo on the social structure of the people of the Intermountain area. This is in itself surprising, for a great deal of conjecture has revolved around just this question, but in the course of research upon the societies of the Plains proper. Such inquiry has often attempted to compare Plains societies of the horse period with those of the pre-horse era, revealed through archaeology and ethnohistory. In this volume, we attempt to approach the problem through both ethnohistory and a type of controlled comparison. That is, using the mounted, buffalo-hunting Shoshone and Bannock as our example, we will relate their social and economic life not only to the Plains, but to the Basin-Plateau area to the west and to their unmounted colinguists who resided there. In this way, we may analyze similarities and differences and attempt to answer the question of whether certain basic social modifications did indeed follow from the buffalo hunt.

The Indian inhabitants of western Wyoming and southeastern Idaho, the subjects of this study, have their closest linguistic affinities with the peoples to the west. The languages of this area are well known and we need only briefly recapitulate their relationships. Those peoples of the Basin-Plateau area known in the ethnographic literature as Shoshone, Gosiute, Northern Paiute, Bannock, Ute, and Southern Paiute all belong to the Uto-Aztecan linguistic stock and are thus related to the Hopi and Aztec to the south and the Comanche of the southern Plains. Within this larger grouping a number of subfamilies have been identified. Those with which this report is concerned are the Shoshone-Comanche and Mono-Bannock. The Shoshone-speaking peoples of the Basin-Plateau area include the Northern, Eastern, and Western Shoshone and the Gosiute, all of whom speak mutually intelligible dialects. The area occupied by this population extends from the Missouri waters on the east to beyond Austin, Nevada, on the west, and from the Sawtooth Mountains of Idaho to southern California. There are no sharp linguistic divisions within this vast region, and phonemic shifts are gradual throughout its extent. The Mono-Bannock division comprehends the speakers of Northern Paiute living in the region east of the Sierra Nevada from Owens Lake, California, to northeastern Oregon and the Bannock Indians of southeastern Idaho, who stem directly from the eastern Oregon Paiute.

Despite the continuity of language between the Shoshone and Bannock of Wyoming and Idaho and the simple Basin people to the west, it has long been obvious that the first two were culturally marginal to the Plains. Wissler listed the Northern and Eastern Shoshone and the Bannock among the Plains tribes, but he excluded them from his category of groups typical of the area and described them as "intermediate" (Wissler, 1920, pp. 19-20). Kroeber, however, was more aware of the historical recency of Plains culture and described the Idaho Bannock and Shoshone and the Wind River (Eastern) Shoshone as forming "marginal subareas" of the Basin (Kroeber, 1939, p. 53). As such, they are included in his Intermediate and Intermountain Areas. Kroeber noted specifically of the Eastern Shoshone (p. 80):

> These people, in turn, live in an area which belongs to the Rocky Mountains physiographically, with the Basin vegetationally: it is sagebrush, not grassland. Wind River culture must have been of pretty pure Basin type until the horse came in and they began to take on an overlay of Plains culture. It was about this time, apparently, that the Comanche moved south from them.

Shimkin, who made an intensive study of the Eastern Shoshone of the Wind River Reservation, is inclined to emphasize their Plains affiliation (1947a, p. 245):

> Wind River Shoshone culture has been essentially that of the Plains for a good two hundred years; pioneer ethnographers have vastly overemphasized the Basin affiliations.

Assuming that this 200-year period dates approximately from the time of Shimkin's field work in 1937-1938, this would extend the Plains cultural position of the Shoshone back to the time at which the Blackfoot were just acquiring horses, a period in which the use of the horse had yet to reach the tribes north and east of the Missouri River (Haines, 1938, pp. 433-435). Although Shimkin rightly states (1939) that the Shoshone were among the earliest mounted buffalo hunters of the northern Plains, it is most questionable whether one can speak of a "Plains culture" at that time, in the sense that the term has been used in culture area classifications. It would seem that the resolution of this problem depends upon the questions of the degree of stability of Plains culture and of the extent to which it is autochthonous to the Plains.

Implicit in the discussions above is the attempt to ascertain whether the buffalo-hunting Shoshone were one thing or another-as if the alternatives constituted in themselves homogeneous units-or how much their culture was a blend. Hultkrantz has taken a rather different approach to the problem in his statement (1949, p. 157):

The conclusion is that the culture of the Wind River Shoshoni exhibits a strange conflicting situation. It belongs neither to the foodgatherers of the west nor to the hunting cultures of the east-it is something sui generis. To ascribe it to anyone of its bordering cultures is to lose the dynamic aspect of the cultural evolution of the tribe.

He thus sees the eastern Shoshone as synthesizers and transformers of cultural material derived from both eastern and western sources; their culture is a blend of the two, but it is not a simple compound of them. The present work does not attempt to answer the question of the relation of the content of the culture of the equestrian Shoshone to that of peoples to the east and west but will focus attention upon social structure. And it will do this, not through a consideration of outside influences upon the Shoshone, but by analysis of their social institutions and the relationship of them to economic life.

Our note on the length of involvement of the Shoshone in Plains Indian culture leads us to inquire briefly into the time depth of this culture and its relation to the expansion of the American frontier. Although it is quite probable that certain cultural traits and social institutions characteristic of later Plains life had antecedents in the pre-equestrian period, the possession of herds of horses was the basis of later patterns of amalgamation and incipient stratification. It also had much to do with the intensification of warfare. The horse, according to Haines (1938), spread from the Spanish Southwest to more northerly areas along both sides of the Rocky Mountains. Its diffusion along the western slope of the range was presumably the more rapid, and Haines gives evidence indicating that the Shoshone had horses about 1690 to 1700, at which time the animal was found no farther north than the Arkansas-Oklahoma border in the Plains (ibid., p. 435). From this Shoshone center, the use of the horse spread north to the Columbia River, the Plateau, and the northern plains. It followed an independent route north from Texas to the Missouri River and the fringe of the woodlands.

Their early acquisition of the horse may have allowed the Shoshone to penetrate the northern plains as far as Saskatchewan in the early eighteenth century, for David Thompson's journals tell of warfare between the Blackfoot and Shoshone in that region at some time in the 1720's or early 1730's (Tyrell, 1916, pp. 328 ff.). The northerly extension of the Shoshone in the early horse period, and perhaps before, has been discussed and generally accepted by many students of the area (cf. Wissler, 1910, p. 17; Shimkin, 1939, p. 22; Ewers, 1955, pp. 16-17; Hultkrantz, 1958, p. 150). There is little information on Shoshone population movements between this date and the journey of Lewis and Clark. In 1742 the de la Vérendrye brothers undertook an expedition into the northern plains of the United States and reported upon the ferocity of a people known to them as the "Gens du Serpent," presumably the Snake, or Shoshone. De la Vérendrye wrote of these people (Margry, 1888, p. 601):

No nation is their friend. We are told that in 1741 they entirely laid waste to seventeen villages, killed all the men and old women, made slaves of the young women and traded them to the sea for horses and merchandise.

The Gens du Serpent are not precisely located, but the explorers were told by the "Gens de Chevaux" that they lie in the path to the western sea. Later, a "Gens d'Arc" chief invited them to join in an expedition against the Gens du Serpent on "the slopes of the great mountains that are near the sea" (p. 603). They later found an abandoned enemy village near the mountains, but returned without further contact. Shimkin believes that this village was in the Black Hills (Shimkin, 1939, p. 22), but the journals are most hazy on geography. The previously cited information from the Gens d'Arc chief suggests that the group was located farther west, in the vicinity of the Rocky Mountains. It must be remembered, however, that there has been considerable contention among historians, not only over the route of the de la Vérendrye brothers, but over the identification of the Gens du Serpent. L. J. Burpee has reviewed (1927, pp. 13-23) various conflicting interpretations of the journals, and the matter can hardly be considered settled.

By this period, the Blackfoot and other northern tribes were already armed with guns (see Ewers, 1955, p. 16; Haines, 1938, p. 435), obtained through commerce with the French and English traders of Canada. They had also become mounted, and it may be surmised that the Shoshone lost their equestrian advantage at almost the same time that their enemies acquired guns. Thus the Shoshone retreat from the Canadian plains may well have begun before 1750, as Thompson's narrative indeed suggests (Tyrrell, 1916, pp. 334 ff.). The process was certainly complete by 1805, when Lewis and Clark found the Lemhi River Shoshone hiding in the fastnesses west of the Bitterroot Range and lamenting their loss of the Missouri River buffalo country to better-armed groups. The Shoshone, once masters of the northern Plains, had fallen upon bad times. They complained to the explorers that they were forced to reside on the waters of the Columbia River from the middle of May to the first of September for fear of the Blackfoot, who had driven them out of the buffalo country with firearms (Lewis and Clark, 1904-06, 2:373). Their forays into the Missouri drainage were made only in strength with other Shoshone and their Flathead allies (2:374). The Shoshone apparently were able to utilize areas of Montana adjacent to the Bitterroot Range, for signs of their root-digging activities were seen on the Beaverhead River (2:329-334). This pattern of transmontane buffalo hunting described by Lewis and Clark remained essentially the same until its final end after the establishment of the reservation, and will be described in detail later in this work.

It is possible now to discern three periods in this early phase of Shoshone history. The first, the footgoing period, is unknown, and little can be inferred of Shoshone location and movements. The second period is characterized by the acquisition of the horse, and we would conjecture that a good deal of territorial expansion took place after that time. The Comanche differentiated from the main Shoshone group at the beginning of the eighteenth century. Although the Comanche maintained communication with their northern colinguists, the territories of the two groups were not contiguous by the end of the century, and their histories followed separate courses. The extension of the Shoshone into the northern Plains may possibly have predated the acquisition of the horse, for it seems quite likely that they occupied fairly extensive areas east of the Rockies in the footgoing period. But, on the other hand, it seems unlikely that in the period immediately preceding 1700, the most probable date for the acquisition of the horse, they extended from the Arkansas River on the south to the Bow River in Saskatchewan. This would be especially unlikely if later distribution of Shoshone-speakers in the Basin-Plateau was substantially the same in the earlier period also. We would conjecture, then, that equestrian life gave the Shoshone the mobility to extend into the Canadian buffalo grounds but that they were pushed back beyond the divide well before 1800. As Shimkin has noted, the ravages of smallpox and the resulting decline of population probably contributed to their territorial shrinkage (Shimkin, 1939, p. 22).

By 1810, the early explorations of Thompson, Lewis and Clark, and others bore fruit in the commercial exploitation of the far Northwest. The fur trade had already reached the Plains and the Rockies in Canada, and a fierce competition was being waged by the Hudson's Bay Fur Company and the North West Company for the patronage of the Indians there. The British interests pushed southward from Canada, and in 1809 David Thompson established North West Company trading posts on Pend Oreille Lake at the mouth of the Clark Fork River and another farther up that stream within the borders of present-day Montana. At the same time, American traders were pushing westward, and Andrew Henry crossed the Continental Divide to locate his trading post on Henry's Fork of the Snake River in 1810. Also, John Jacob Astor's Pacific Fur Company established the ill-fated Astoria post at the mouth of the Columbia River in 1811. Although this particular American enterprise foundered, Manuel Lisa, the guiding spirit of the Missouri Fur Company, penetrated the Missouri River country and founded a post on the Yellowstone River at the mouth of the Big Horn in 1807. From this point his trappers spread into the near-by mountain country. The most famous of these mountain men was John Colter, who trapped the country of the Blackfoot and Crow and discovered Yellowstone Park.

The northern Plains and Rockies had thus been entered and partially explored by 1812, and increasing numbers of trappers poured into the new Louisiana Purchase and the lands beyond. Astor stepped into the territory of the Missouri Fur Company after Lisa's death in 1820, and in 1822 the Western Division of his American Fur Company was established. Fort Union was built on the upper Missouri to serve as the headquarters of Astor's mountain realm, and steamboats served the post after 1832. A decade before this date, the Rocky Mountain Fur Company was established, and in the following year, 1823, the company's trappers began to exploit intensively the drainages of the Wind River and the upper Snake and Green rivers. The Rocky Mountain Company established a new pattern of trading. Eschewing the rigid and hierarchical organization of the British companies, it relied mainly upon the services of free trappers, who gathered once a year at agreed places to meet the company's supply trains. These gatherings, the famous trappers' rendezvous, were held in the summer at various places in Shoshone country-Pierre's Hole, Cache Valley, or the Green River.

The trappers of the Rocky Mountain Company and later of the American Fur Company invested every fastness of the Shoshone hunting grounds in relentless pursuit of the beaver, the vital ingredient of the gentleman's top hat. The intense traffic in the Shoshone region was abetted by the penetration of the Snake River drainage by Donald McKenzie of the North West Company, beginning in 1818, and later by Peter Skene Ogden, under the auspices of the Hudson's Bay Company. The climax of fur trapping came in the middle of the decade of the 1830's, for at the peak of activity the commerce collapsed. Competition between the various trading companies had been ruinous, the streams had been thoroughly trapped out, and the beaver hat went out of fashion. By 1840, the fur trade in the northwest part of the United States was substantially ended.

During the period 1810-1840 the Shoshone and their neighbors lost the isolation they had formerly enjoyed and came into close contact with the whites. The latter were of a different type than those with whom the Indians later had to deal. They lived off the land, but at the same time they did not dispossess the Indians from their hunting grounds. Although there were sporadic clashes between the trappers and Shoshone and Bannock groups, relations were largely amicable. The trappers married Indian women and lived for varying periods with Indian bands. And both found a common enemy in the Blackfoot. The Indians also traded with the whites and through them obtained firearms, iron utensils, and other commodities, including the raw liquor of the frontier. But the American companies apparently did not attempt to utilize Indian labor to the same extent as did the British companies. The bulk of the fur yield was garnered by the free trappers and not by Indians. The Shoshone traded some small animal furs and buffalo robes to the whites, but they also sold meat, horses, and other commodities. They never became fur trappers in the same complete way as did the northern Algonkian and Athapaskan peoples.

After the decline of the fur trade, the Shoshone did not return to their pristine state of isolation. In the early 1840's, shortly after the debacle of the beaver trade, a strong surge of immigration from the States to Oregon began. The road to Oregon followed trails well marked by the trappers. It ascended the Platte and North Platte rivers and thence to the South Pass via the Sweetwater. From South Pass the trail went down to Fort Bridger, established in 1843, and then turned to the northwest and Fort Hall on the Snake River. The California branch of the trail bent southwest before reaching Fort Hall and descended the Humboldt River. The initial trickle of emigration grew into a great stream, and after the discovery of gold in California the Oregon Trail became a great highway to the west.

Busy though the trail was, the emigrants had but a single purpose. This was to cross the "Great American Desert," or the Plains, and reach the promised lands of the Pacific Coast. Except for the immediate environs of the emigrant road, the mountain country contained fewer whites than during the previous decade. This situation soon changed. In 1847 the Mormon migration reached the Salt Lake Valley, and during the following years Mormons settled adjacent areas of Wyoming and Idaho. Miners poured into the Sweetwater River country of Wyoming in the 1860's and in 1869 Fort Stambaugh was established at South Pass to protect them and the emigrant road. This route, however, had already seen its greatest days, for the Central Pacific Railroad was completed in the same year.

The Wild West was substantially ended by this date, and the Shoshone signed treaties in 1868 which gave those of Wyoming the Wind River Reservation and those of Idaho the Fort Hall Reservation. Sedentarization of these buffalo-hunting nomads was completed during the 1870's, by which time the region was being settled by white ranchers and their Texas herds. Shortly after 1880, the buffalo herds had been almost completely exterminated, and so also had Plains Indian life.

The era from 1700 to 1880 was thus one of great change for the Shoshone. We recapitulate its principal periods.

1. The pre-horse period extended until approximately 1700.

2. The early equestrian period, from 1700 to 1750 was distinguished by the expansion of Shoshone-speaking peoples into the Canadian plains to the north and southward toward Texas, where they became known as Comanche.

3. After 1750, the northern tribes, especially the Blackfoot, acquired the horse and firearms and drove the Shoshone south and west, where they retreated beyond the Continental Divide, in contiguity with those Shoshone who had remained in the Great Basin. By this time, the Comanche had become differentiated from their northern colinguists.

4. The fur period began about 1810, and from this time, Shoshone history became inextricably connected with that of the American frontiers. Although the game supply declined during this epoch, the Shoshone were not dispossessed from their hunting grounds and continued substantially the same subsistence cycle.

5. The year 1840 saw the end of the fur trade and the beginning of westward emigration. As will be seen, the buffalo herds west of the Divide had disappeared by this date, and the Shoshone were increasingly forced to seek winter supplies on the Missouri waters.

6. The Shoshone signed treaties in 1868 in which they were forced to accept reservation life. At about this time, gold miners entered the Sweetwater country, and the transcontinental railroad was completed. The following decade saw the end of the buffalo in the west and the introduction of open-range cattle grazing. Shoshone history then became merged with the history of the American West.

During the periods of the fur trade and early emigration increasing amounts of information on Shoshonean and Mono-Bannock speakers became available. Political organization among these peoples was characteristically amorphous, and the early diarists and chroniclers had little basis for distinguishing subgroups in this vast region. With the exception of the Paiute-Shoshone split, language differences gave no firm basis for differentiation, and even this major division of the Uto-Aztecan stock was commonly not recognized. Accordingly, travelers classified the Indians of the region on the basis of their most obvious characteristic, whether or not they possessed horses and hunted buffalo. Alexander Ross observed (1924, pp. 239-240):

> The great Snake nation may be divided into three divisions, namely, the Shirry-dikas, or dog-eaters; the War-are-ree-kas, or fish-eaters; and the Ban-at-tees, or robbers; but as a nation they all go by the general appellation of Sho-sho-nes, or Snakes. The word Sho-sho-nes means, in the Snake language, "inland." The Snakes, on the west side of the Rocky Mountains, are what the Sioux are on the east side-the most numerous and powerful in the country. The Shirry-dikas are the real Sho-sho-nes, and live in the plains, hunting the buffalo. They are generally slender, but tall, well-made, rich in horses, good warriors, well dressed, clean in their camps, and in their personal appearance bold and independent.

The War-are-ree-kas are very numerous, but neither united nor formidable. They live chiefly by fishing, and are to be found all along the rivers, lakes, and water-pools throughout the country. They are more corpulent, slovenly, and indolent than the Shirry-dikas. Badly armed and badly clothed, they seldom go to war. Dirty in their camp, in their dress, and in their persons, they differed so far in their general habits from the Shirry-dikas that they appeared as if they had been people belonging to another country. These are the defenceless wretches whom the Blackfeet and Piegans from beyond the mountains generally make war upon. These foreign mercenaries carry off the scalps and women of the defenseless War-are-ree-kas and the horses of the Shirry-dikas, but are never formidable nor bold enough to attack the latter in fair and open combat.

The Ban-at-tees, or mountain Snakes, live a predatory and wandering life in the recesses of the mountains, and are to be found in small bands or single wigwams among the caverns and rocks. They are looked upon by the real Sho-sho-nes themselves as outlaws, their hand against every man, and every man's hand against them. They live chiefly by plunder. Friends and foes are alike to them. They generally frequent the northern frontiers, and other mountainous parts of the country. In summer they go almost naked, but during winter they clothe themselves with the skins of rabbits, wolves, and other animals.

Ross's "Ban-at-tees" undoubtedly include the people now termed the Northern Paiute of Oregon; this seems confirmed by his placement of the western limits of the "Snakes" at the western end of the Blue Mountain Range in Oregon. The loose inclusion of the Oregon Northern Paiute as Snakes results in some obscurity in the early sources. They are frequently (and on valid linguistic grounds) lumped with the Bannock, as was done by Ross. It is noteworthy that contemporary Fort Hall informants still speak of the Oregon Paiute as Bannocks.

The distinction between mounted and unmounted peoples continues in Zenas Leonard's journal (1934, p. 80):

The Snake Indians, or as some call them, the Shoshonie, were once a powerful nation, possessing a glorious hunting ground on the east side of the [Rocky] mountains; but they, like the Flatheads, have been almost annihilated by the revengeful Blackfeet, who, being supplied with firearms, were enabled to defeat all Indian opposition. Their nation had been entirely broken up and scattered throughout all this wild region. The Shoshonies are a branch of the once powerful Snake tribe, as are also the more abject and forlorn tribe of Shuckers, or, more generally termed, Diggers and Root-eaters, who keep in the most retired recesses of the mountains and streams, subsisting on the most unwholesome food, and living the most like animals of any race of beings.

Russell also commented that half the Shoshone live in large villages and hunt buffalo, while the other half travel in small groups of two to ten families, have few horses, and live on roots, fish, seeds, and berries (Russell, 1955, p. 143). Wilkes follows this same dichotomy (1845, 4:471-472):

The Snakes, or Shoshones, are widely scattered tribes, and some even assert that they are of the same race as the Comanches, whose separation is said to be remembered by the Snakes: it has been ascertained, in confirmation of this opinion, that they both speak the same language. The hunters report that the proper country of the Snakes is to the east of Youta Lake and north of the Snake or Lewis River; but they are found in many detached places. The largest band is located near Fort Boise on the Snake River, to the north of the Bonacks. The Snakes have horses and firearms, and derive their subsistence both from the chase and from fishing. There are other bands of them, to the north of the Bonacks, who have no horses, and live on acorns and roots, their only arms being bows and arrows. In consequence of the mode of gaining their subsistence, they are called Diggers and are looked upon with great contempt.

Wilkes further commented (p. 473) that there had been a general north-to-south tribal pressure in which the Blackfoot had occupied former Shoshone lands: "the country now in possession of the Snakes, belonged to the Bonacks, who have been driven to the Sandy Desert."

Father De Smet reported that the "Shoshonees or Root-diggers" had a population of 10,000, divided into "several parties" (De Smet, 1906, 27:163). The missionary claimed they were called Snakes because they burrowed into the earth and lived on roots, and commented (ibid.):

They would have no other food if some hunting parties did not occasionally pass beyond the mountains in pursuit of the buffalo, while a part of the tribe proceeds along the banks of the Salmon River, to make provision for the winter, at the season when the fish come up from the sea.

Albert Gallatin described the various Shoshone populations and their orbits in 1848, as follows (Hale, 1848, p. 18):

Shoshonees or Snake Indians ... bounded north by Sahaptins, west by the Waiilatpu, Lutuami, and Palaiks; extend eastwardly east of the Rocky Mountains.... The country of the Shoshonees proper is east of Snake River. The Western Shoshonees, or Wihinasht, live west of it; and between them and the Shoshonees proper, another branch of the same family, called Ponasht or Bonnaks, occupy both sides of the Snake River and the valley of its tributary, the Owyhee. The Eastern Shoshonees are at war with the Blackfeet and the Opsarokas. The most northern of these have no horses, live on acorns and roots, are called diggers, and considered by our hunters the most miserable of the Indians.

Gallatin's division is the first, to our knowledge, to apply the terms Eastern and Western Shoshone.

In Schoolcraft's Archives of Aboriginal Knowledge the Shoshone are described in terms consistent with previously published material (1860, 1:198):

The various tribes and bands of Indians of the Rocky Mountains, south of latitude 43°, who are known under this general name [Shoshonee], occupy the elevated area of the Utah basin. They embrace all the territory of the Great South Pass between the Mississippi Valley and the waters of the Columbia.... Traces of them, in this latitude, are first found in ascending the Sweetwater River of the north fork of the Platte, or Nebraska. They spread over the sources of the Green River ... on the summit south of the Great Wind river chain of mountains, and thence westward, by the Bear river valley, to and down the Snake river, or Lewis fork of the Columbia. Under the name of Yampa-tick-ara, or Root-Eaters, and Bonacks, they occupy, with the Utahs, the vast elevated basin of the Great Salt Lake, extending south and west to the borders of New Mexico and California.... They extend down the Sä-ap-tin or Snake River valley, to north of latitude 44°, but this is not the limit to which the nations speaking the Shoshonee language in its several dialects, have spread. Ethnologically, the people speaking it are one of the primary stocks of the Rocky Mountain chain.

Other general descriptions of the Shoshonean-speaking peoples of the Basin and Rocky Mountain areas are found in the literature of the period, but add little to the foregoing accounts, which give us a picture of a population sharing a common language (except the Bannock) and living in peaceful relations with one another. They were roughly divided into mounted and unmounted populations located in the eastern and western parts of the territory, respectively. While the mounted people appeared to have had some degree of political cohesion and military effectiveness, the "Diggers" are uniformly represented as politically atomistic, impoverished, and weak in the face of their enemies.

Since a work of this type relies heavily upon identification of peoples mentioned in historical sources, it would be well to review the varying nomenclature applied to the Shoshone.

Most early writers designated the Shoshonean-speaking population as "Shoshonees" or "Snake Indians." The term "Snake" was generally applied indiscriminately to the Northern Paiute of Oregon and to Bannock and Shoshone groups in southern Idaho. Frequently only the mounted people were considered true "Snakes," as in Wilkes's statement that "the proper country of the Snakes is to the east of the Youta Lake and north of the Snake or Lewis River; but they are found in many detached places" (Wilkes, 1845, 4:471). He goes on to say (p. 472) that some Snakes have no horses, but these he locates north of the Bannock.

Although de la Vérendrye's "Gens du Serpent" can only be presumed to be Shoshone, there is little doubt that the "Snake" of whom Thompson's Blackfoot informant spoke were Shoshone. Lewis and Clark were told by the Indians of the Columbia River that they lived in fear of the "Snake Indians," but this was in reference to a tribe of the Deschutes River in central Oregon (Lewis and Clark, 1904-06, 3:147). Those Indians whom they met on the Lemhi River in Idaho were, however, termed "Shoshonees." The name, "Snake," was rapidly applied to almost any Indians between South Pass and the Columbia River. In March, 1826, Peter Skene Ogden reported a "Snake" camp of two hundred on the Raft River (Ogden, 1909, 10 (4):357). These Indians were undoubtedly either Shoshone or Bannock, as their location indicates. Nathaniel Wyeth traveled in the Raft River country in August, 1832, and similarly spoke of seeing "Snakes" (Wyeth, 1899, p. 164). Without making any sharp distinctions between the Indians sighted, Wyeth, in the same region, mentioned "Diggers" (pp. 164, 167), "Pawnacks" (p. 168), and "So-honees" (ibid.). In 1839, Farnham saw "a family of Root Digger Indians" on the Snake River, near the mouth of Raft River (Farnham, 1843, p. 74). These Indians were no doubt Shoshone, but the term was also applied to Northern Paiute, for Ogden encountered "Snakes" while on a trapping expedition in the Harney Basin of Oregon in 1826 (Ogden, 1910, 11 (2):206), as did John Work six years later (Work, 1945, p. 6). The failure to recognize the Northern Paiute as being linguistically distinct from the Shoshone continued for some time. In 1854, Indian Agent Thompson reported from the Oregon Territory that among the Indians under his jurisdiction were "Sho-sho-nies," who were divided into three major groups: the "Mountain Snakes," "Bannacks," and "Diggers" (Thompson, 1855, p. 493).

North of the present boundary of the state of Nevada, "Snake" and "Shoshone" or variations thereof were the names commonly applied to all the Indians. Frequently, "Snake" meant specifically Paiute and Bannock, or any mounted Indians, as distinguished from the footgoing "Diggers." From the fact that these terms were applied to Indians in widely separated regions and having different languages, it can only be concluded that the nomenclature designated no particular group having political, cultural, or linguistic unity.

"Snake" was but infrequently applied to the Indians south of Oregon and Idaho, where the term "Shoshone" was more widely used. The unmounted Shoshonean-speaking peoples of Utah and Nevada were also commonly referred to as "Diggers" or "Root Diggers," a name frequently given to the unmounted Shoshone of Idaho. Washington Irving referred to those Indians seen on the Humboldt River by Walker's party in 1833 as "Shoshokoes" (Irving, 1873, p. 384). Zenas Leonard, who was a member of Walker's expedition, referred to the Indians of the Humboldt River region as "Bawnack, or Shoshonies" (Leonard, 1934, p. 78), but Father De Smet spoke of all the unmounted people of the Great Basin as "Soshocos" and described their abject poverty (De Smet, 1905, 3:1032). In 1846, Edwin Bryant entered the Great Basin en route to California. Of the Shoshone he said: "The Shoshonees or Snakes occupy the country immediately west of the South Pass of the Rocky Mountains" (Bryant, 1885, p. 137). He differentiated this powerful, mounted people from the "miserable Digger Indians, calling themselves Soshonees," whom he met west of Great Salt Lake (p. 168). As he continued down the Humboldt River in Nevada, he noted: "All the Digger Indians of this valley claim to be Shoshonees" (p. 195), but despite this affirmation, he continued to refer to them as "Diggers." Similarly, two Indians met by Bryant's party near Humboldt Sink in Northern Paiute territory were called "Digger Indians" (p. 211). Howard Stansbury, who explored the Great Salt Lake region in 1849, referred, however, to the Indians west of the lake as "Shoshonees or Snake Indians" (Stansbury, 1852, p. 97).

The Western Shoshone were generally called "Diggers" by the emigrants who took part in the gold rush to California. One of them, Franklin Langworthy of Illinois, stated: "All the Indians along the Humboldt call themselves Shoshonees, but the whites call them Diggers, from the fact that they burrow under ground in the winter" (Langworthy, 1932, p. 119). Reuben Shaw, another "Forty-niner," referred to the Indians on the California road along the Humboldt as "Diggers" (Shaw, 1948, p. 123), "Root Diggers" (p. 119), and "Humboldt Indians" (p. 130). In 1854 Lieutenant E. G. Beckwith explored the route of the forty-first parallel in search of a possible railroad route and encountered Gosiute, Western Shoshone, and Northern Paiute Indians. He referred to all of them as "Diggers," and he apparently used this term generically for all the impoverished, horseless Indians between Salt Lake City and the Sierra Nevada Mountains. At Deep Creek, in Utah, he "found a band of twenty Shoshonee Indians encamped, besides women and children. They are mounted, and contrast strikingly with their Goshoot neighbors (Diggers) ..." (Beckwith, 1855, p. 25). Beckwith classed only mounted Indians as Shoshone: in Butte Valley, Nevada, the inhabitants of a "Digger wick-e-up" fled from the party, "taking us for Shoshonees" (p. 26). After leaving Western Shoshone territory he spoke of "Digger Indians, who call themselves Pah-Utah, however" (p. 34).

The name "Shoshone" became more commonly applied to the Western Shoshone after they had had increased contact with the whites. The French traveler, Jules Remy, spoke of them as "Shoshones, or Snakes" in 1855 (Remy and Brenchley, 1861, p. 123), and the British explorer, Richard Burton, distinguished the "Shoshone" from the "Gosh-Yuta" (Burton, 1861, p. 567) and the "Pa Yuta," or Northern Paiute, in 1860 (p. 591). The term "Shoshonee" was applied by Indian Agent Holeman to the Indians of Thousand Spring Valley, Nevada (Holeman, 1854, p. 443), and to those of the Humboldt River (p. 444); However, on Willow Creek, Utah, Agent Garland Hurt met a group of mounted Indians whom he called "Shoshonees, or Snakes proper, from the Green River country" (Hurt, 1856, p. 517). He distinguished these from the "Diggers" of the Humboldt River (p. 779). Thus the distinction between the mounted Shoshone and the unmounted people of the more arid regions of the Great Basin continued, despite the recognition of their unity of language. This implicit recognition may be found in the statement made by Brigham Young (1858, p. 599):

> The Shoshones are not hostile to travelers, so far as they inhabit this territory, except perhaps a few called "Snake diggers," who inhabit, as before stated, along the line of travel west of the settlements.

It is possible to document almost endlessly the ways in which the labels "Shoshone," "Digger," and "Snake" were applied in turn or at the same time to Shoshone-Comanche and Mono-Bannock speakers alike. Since political or social significance has frequently been attributed to Indians' names-both those bestowed by the whites and those by which the several sectors of the Shoshone population referred to each other-we will discuss this nomenclature in the context of each section of the following report.

―――――――――――――――――

II. THE EASTERN SHOSHONE

It is necessary to preface all discussions of Shoshone Indians with a clarification of what is implied by the names attached to Shoshone subgroups. The commonly used appellation "Wind River Shoshone" implies no more than reservation membership. Thus, we also have "Owyhee Shoshone" and "Fort Hall Shoshone" (and Bannock). Wind River residents of admitted descent from other groups are also referred to as "Wind River people," if they are on the agency rolls. They were, of course, not known by this name or a native equivalent in the pre-reservation period. The names, "Eastern Shoshones" and "Eastern Snakes," by which the Shoshone of Wyoming are also known in anthropology, were first consistently applied by government officials during the 1850's and 1860's (cf. Lander, 1860, p. 131; Head, 1868, p. 179; Mann, 1869, p. 616). Lander also referred to the Eastern Shoshone as the "Wash-i-kee band of the Snake Indians" (Lander, 1859, p. 66). This term came into common use after Chief Washakie rose to prominence in the eyes of the whites.

Previous to this period the Eastern Shoshone were called Snakes and Shoshones (or variations thereof), indiscriminately. As has been mentioned, the only firm distinction was made according to whether or not the Indians in question owned horses and hunted buffalo. Although Lewis and Clark never visited the Wyoming lands, the tribal lists which they compiled at Fort Mandan before pushing west mention a group, said by Clark to be "Snake," called the "Cas-ta-ha-na" or "Gens de Vache" (Lewis and Clark, 1904-06, 6:102). They were said to number 500 lodges having a population of about 5,000 people. The Shoshone identity of this people is somewhat obscured by Clark's report of an affinity between their language and that of the Minitaree, but, on the other hand, they were said to "rove on a S. E. fork of the Yellow Rock River called Big Horn, and the heads of the Loup" (ibid.). The "Cas-ta-ha-na" are mentioned also during the return trip of the expedition. Lewis and Clark noted of the Big Horn River: "It is inhabited by a great number of roving Indians of the Crow Nation, the paunch Nation (a band of Crows) and the Castahanas (a band of Snake In.)." The editor of the journals, Reuben Thwaites, identifies the latter as "Comanche." (Ibid., 5:297.)

The paucity of boundary nomenclature found in the historical sources is continued in the ethnographic data, for the food-area terminology used by the Nevada and Idaho Shoshone is even more diffusely applied in Wyoming. One old Nevada Shoshone woman referred to the Eastern Shoshone as Kwichundöka, while a native of Wind River referred to his people as Gwichundöka, slight phonetic variants of the common term meaning "Buffalo eaters." This name appears in Hoebel (1938, p. 413) as Kutsindika. Hoebel also reports that the Idaho Shoshone referred to the Wyoming people as Pohogani, "Sage Brush Home" and Kogohoii, "Gut Eaters" (ibid.). (Hoebel's terms are here anglicized.)

Whatever names may be applied to identify the Shoshone of Wyoming, none refer to any sort of political group maintaining a stable territory. As Shimkin says (1947*a*, p. 246):

> The identification of the Wind River Shoshone and their territory is not a simple matter. It is complicated by several facts. These people had no developed national or tribal sense; affiliation was fluid. Nor did they distinguish themselves by a special name. They merely knew that others called them ... Sage Brushers, ... Sage Brush Homes, or ... Buffalo Eating People. Furthermore, they felt no clear-cut distinctions of private or tribal territories.

One may speak of an eastern population of Shoshone Indians, but it would be inaccurate to speak of one Eastern Shoshone band, despite the fact that leadership was better developed in Wyoming than in other parts of Shoshone territory.

It is doubtful whether there was any accurate estimate of the Eastern Shoshone population until the post-reservation period. Burton (1861, p. 575) cited the no doubt exaggerated figure of 12,000 for the population led by Washakie. Forney numbers the total Shoshone population at 4,500 in 1859 (1860*a*, p. 733), while Doty raised this to 8,650 in 1863 (1865, p. 320). The more reliable estimate of 1,600 Eastern Shoshone was given by Agent Mann in 1869 (1870, p. 715), after the establishment of the Wind River reservation. This number was later reduced to 1,250 in official reports (Patten, 1878, p. 646). Kroeber has estimated the Wind River Shoshone population at 2,500 (1939, p. 137). These figures are not representative of earlier periods, for the ravages of smallpox and other new diseases made heavy inroads on the pre-treaty population, and it is probable that the population at the time of the treaty did not greatly exceed 1,500.

EASTERN SHOSHONE HISTORY: 1800-1875

According to Shoshone tradition, the winter camps of the Eastern Shoshone were in the valley of the Wind River, and their hunting territory extended north to Yellowstone Park and Cody and east to the Big Horn Mountains and beyond South Pass. Little is said by informants of excursions west of the Continental Divide, although historical evidence suggests that this was actually once their principal hunting grounds. In partial support of this contention, Shimkin says (1947*a*, p. 247): "The historical evidence gives some weight to the assumption that in 1835-1840 the Shoshones were mostly west of the Wind River Mountains." He also notes that hostilities between the Shoshone and Crow resulted in the westward withdrawal of the former again in the 1850's (ibid.). In an earlier article Shimkin also stated (1938, p. 415):

> This [smallpox epidemics in the first half of the 19th century], and probably the increased aggressiveness of other Plains tribes with the spread of firearms as well, led to a recession of the Shoshone and their retreat to the west in the middle of the nineteenth century. A final wave of expansion onto the Plains came with white aid, following the treaty at Fort Bridger, July 3, 1868.

While agreeing in part with these conclusions, we would not confine the Shoshone restriction to the territory west of the Continental Divide to such limited periods. The following data suggest, rather, that "the heart of this people's territory," as Shimkin describes the Wind River country, did not extend west of the Wind River Range from at least 1800 until the reservation period and that the Shoshone, while frequently entering the Missouri River drainage, did so only for brief periods and usually in considerable fear of attack.

In Washington Irving's account of the Astoria party, one of our earliest reliable sources on the Wyoming Shoshone, the author tells how the Shoshone were pushed out of the Missouri River buffalo country after the North West and Hudson's Bay Companies put firearms in the hands of the Blackfoot (Irving, 1890, p. 197):

> Thus by degrees the Snakes have become a scattered, broken-spirited, impoverished people, keeping about lonely rivers and mountain streams, and subsisting chiefly upon fish. Such of them as still possess horses and occasionally figure as hunters are called Shoshonies.

The westward-bound Astoria party traveled up the Wind River Valley in the middle of September, 1811, without sighting any Indians (ibid., pp. 199-200). This was exactly the time of year when, according to contemporary informants, the Shoshone buffalo party should have been gathering there. However, on the western side of the Wind River Range, they found "a party of Snakes who had come across the mountains on their autumnal hunting excursion to provide buffalo meat for the winter" (p. 202). In September of the following year, the eastward-bound party under Stuart encountered a party of "Upsarokas, or Crows" on the Bear River, who said that they intended to trade with the Shoshone (p. 289). This Crow party later ran off the trappers' horses. Throughout their trip to the Green River country, the trapping party was in continual fear of the Blackfoot (p. 298). Upon arriving on the Green River on

October 17, 1812, they met a party of about 130 "Snakes" living in some 40 "wigwams" made of pine branches (p. 306). The ostensibly peaceful Crow had run off all but one of the horses of this camp and had stolen some women also. The Astoria chronicle, then, documents a situation that appears consistently in later sources: the Shoshone were usually encountered west of the Continental Divide and were continually on the defensive against powerful tribes to the east and north that seemingly entered their hunting grounds at will.

The activities of the early trappers in northern Utah and western Wyoming brought them into contact with a variety of Indian populations, not all of which are easily identifiable. This region is shown by the reports of the fur seekers to be characterized by a great fluidity of internal movement of Shoshone-and Bannock-speaking groups and by frequent entry by other tribes for purposes of war, trapping, and trade. The journal of J. P. Beckwourth gives a vivid, although not wholly reliable, account of the ebb and flow of population in the area under consideration. While camped near the east shore of the Great Salt Lake late in the year 1823, Beckwourth lost 80 horses to the "Punnaks [Bannocks], a tribe inhabiting the headwaters of the Columbia River" (Beckwourth, 1931, p. 60). His party pursued the Bannock to their village, some five days distant, and, after regaining part of the stolen herd, returned to camp to find some "Snake" (p. 61) (Shoshonean-speaking) Indians camped near by. He states that this group numbered 600 lodges and 2,500 warriors. The Indians were friendly and the locale was said to have been their winter camp (ibid.). Three years later, Beckwourth and his party were camped near the same site (today, Farmington, Utah) and encountered 16 Flathead Indians. Shortly thereafter the trappers were attacked by 500 mounted Blackfoot Indians, who were driven off (ibid., p. 66). Two days later, the fur party was joined by 4,000 Shoshone, who aided them in defeating another Blackfoot attack (pp. 70-71). (Beckwourth's population estimates are probably quite exaggerated.)

While Beckwourth's journals are poorly dated, it was no doubt during the late 1820's that his party was attacked near Salt River in western Wyoming by a body of unidentified Indians who, he claims, were 500 strong (p. 86). Shortly thereafter he fell in with friendly "Snake," or Shoshone, Indians. Near their camp were 185 Bannock lodges, with whose occupants the hunters had some difficulties (pp. 87-88). While in this vicinity, the camp of the trappers and the friendly Shoshone was attacked by a Blackfoot party, after which the trappers and Shoshone moved to the Green River (p. 89). At the Green River camp, the combined trapper-Shoshone group was visited by a party of Crow Indians. Beckwourth comments that "the Snakes and Crows were extremely amicable." Beckwourth reported further on Shoshone-Crow relations (p. 108):

> At this time the Crows were incessantly at war with all the tribes within their reach, with the exception of the Snakes and the Flatheads and they did not escape frequent ruptures with them [over horses].

That this peace was extremely uneasy and manifestly ephemeral was clearly shown by later developments when the Shoshone, accompanied by some Ute, attacked a Crow trading party, which later mustered support and retaliated (pp. 183-184). However, at an even later date Beckwourth was able to report that 200 lodges of Shoshone had joined forces with the Crow, ostensibly because of the trading possibilities afforded by Beckwourth's presence among the latter (p. 249).

The relations between the Shoshone and Crow during the 1820's apparently were not much unlike those that prevailed at the time of the passages of the Astoria parties. The Crow, although not relentless enemies of the Shoshone, as were the Blackfoot, constituted a constant source of danger. Beckwourth's journals give evidence of amicable relations between the American trappers and the Shoshone, although he described the more bellicose Bannock as "very bad Indians, and very great thieves" (p. 87). Other sources document more serious difficulties with "Snake" Indians. Peter Skene Ogden reported in 1826 that the American trappers had suffered severe losses at the hands of the Snake Indians during the preceding three years (Simpson, 1931,

p. 285), but these mishaps probably occurred in Idaho. In 1824, however, Jedediah Smith and Fitzpatrick lost all of their horses to the "Snakes" on the headwaters of the Green River (Alter, 1925, pp. 38-39; Dale, 1918, p. 91), and some members of Etienne Provot's trapping party were killed by "Snakes" in the winter of 1824-25 (Dale, 1918, p. 103).

Little information is available from the eastern side of the Wind River Mountains during the 1820's. We do know, however, that Ashley entrusted his horses to the Crow Indians on the Wind River before setting out for the mountains in the spring of 1824 (ibid., p. 89).

In 1831, an American Fur Company trapper, Warren Angus Ferris, noted that the two main Crow bands were located chiefly on the Yellowstone River and its tributaries, but their "war parties infest the countries of the Eutaws, Snakes, Arrapahoes, Blackfeet, Sious, and Chayennes" (Ferris, 1940, p. 305). He had this to say of the Eastern Shoshone (p. 310):

> Of the Snakes on the plains there are probably about four hundred lodges, six hundred warriors, and eighteen hundred souls. They range in the plains of Green River as far as the Eut Mountains; southward from the source to the outlet of Bear River, of the Big Lake; thence to the mouth of Porto-nuf [Portneuf], on Snake River of the Columbia.... They are at war with the Eutaws, Crows, and Blackfeet, but rob and steal from all their neighbors.

Ferris saw few Indians in his travels through the Jackson Hole area in 1832 and 1833. However, in "Jackson's Little Hole," presumably at the south end of Hoback Canyon, he noted, in August, 1832, several large, abandoned camps, which he assumed were those of the "Grosventres of the prairies" (p. 158). The supposed Gros Ventre party was later seen on the Green River and was said to have consisted of 500 to 600 warriors (pp. 158-159). These may well have been Blackfoot, for Zenas Leonard reported a Blackfoot attack on the upper Snake River in western Wyoming in July, 1832 (Leonard, 1934, p. 51). The Indians most frequently sighted in the Green River region, however, were the Shoshone. In June, 1833, Ferris saw "several squaws scattered over the prairie engaged in digging roots" (Ferris, 1940, p. 205). These women apparently belonged to "some fifty or sixty lodges of Snakes, ...encamped about the fort [Bonneville's] who were daily exchanging their skins and robes, for munitions, knives, ornaments, etc., with the whites" (ibid., p. 206).

Further evidence of the virtual absence of the Shoshone from Missouri waters in the fur period comes from Zenas Leonard. When preparing to spend the winter of 1832-33 on the Green River, the trappers met a party of 70 to 80 Crow who said "they were going to war with the Snake Indians-whose country we were now in-and they said also they belonged to the Crow nation on the East side of the mountains" (Leonard, 1934, pp. 82-83). These Crow stole horses from the party, and the trappers pursued them to their village at the mouth of the Shoshone River, near modern Lovell, Wyoming. In the summer of 1834, Captain Bonneville's trappers, one of whom was Zenas Leonard, trapped on the waters of Wind River, but no mention is made of Shoshone (ibid., pp. 224-226). In October, however, they met the Crow in the Big Horn Basin, and they wintered on Wind River in their company (pp. 255-256). No Shoshone were reported in the area.

The Irving account of Captain Bonneville's adventures contains additional information on Eastern Shoshone settlement patterns. It is here also that we receive our first information on the Shoshone who later are known to us as the Dukarika and who inhabited the mountainous terrain of the Wind River Mountains and adjacent high country (Irving, 1850, p. 139). The journal also supplements Leonard's account of the trappers' sojourn in Wind River Valley, which, Irving wrote (1837, 2:17) was infested by Blackfoot and Crow Indians and was one of the favorite habitats of the latter (p. 22). One of the trapping party's members was taken captive by the Crow on the Popo Agie River, which flows past Lander, Wyoming, but was released unharmed (pp. 24-25). It is to be noted that the trappers were in the Wind River Valley at the end of September but saw no Shoshone, although this was approximately the time of the annual buffalo hunt. Upon leaving Wind River, Bonneville headed for the Sweetwater River, which, he stated, was beyond the limits of Crow country (p. 26). He then went to Hams Fork, a tributary of the Green River, and encountered a Shoshone encampment with the Fitzpatrick party (p. 27).

It is doubtful whether Shoshonean peoples hunted extensively east of the Continental Divide in the period following their eighteenth-century retreat from the northern Plains and before the disappearance of the buffalo west of the Rockies. Although the great herds of the Missouri drainage were not found in the lands inhabited by the Shoshone, it is quite possible that there were sufficient buffalo there to meet the needs of the population. Bonneville met a group of twenty-five mounted Bannock in the neighborhood of Soda Springs, Idaho, in November, 1833, and, at their invitation, joined them in a buffalo hunt there (p. 33). After taking sufficient meat, the Bannock returned to their winter quarters at the mouth of the Portneuf River (p. 35). The winter of 1834-35 again found Bonneville on the Bear River, this time on its upper reaches, where he made winter camp with "a small band of Shoshonies" (p. 210). Farther upstream was an encampment of "Eutaw" Indians, who were hostile to the Shoshone (p. 213). Bonneville, however, managed to prevent conflict between the two groups. One advantage of this winter camp, and a possible source of attraction for the Ute Indians, was the presence of antelope during the winter. Bonneville witnessed one successful "surround" by horsemen, aided in their efforts by supernatural charms reminiscent of Great Basin antelope drives (pp. 214-215).

Nathaniel Wyeth evidently saw few Shoshone in his travels through Wyoming, and his journals do not add greatly to our understanding of the area. He traveled from the Snake to the Green River in June and July, 1832, via the Teton country and mentioned no Shoshone except for a small encampment near Bonneville's post on the upper Green River (Wyeth, 1899, pp. 203-205). However, he reports that a white trapper was attacked in July, 1833, on the lower Wind River by a party of fifteen Shoshone who had left Green River shortly before (p. 207), and, in 1834, he found himself among "too many Indians ... for comfort or safety" while near Hams Fork, Wyoming (p. 225).

The journals of Osborne Russell provide documentation of population movements in Wyoming during the years 1834-1840. Despite the decline of the fur trade during this period, the area was still turbulent. In November, 1834, a party of trappers was reported as having arrived at Fort Hall, Nathaniel Wyeth's new post, after having been routed by the Blackfoot on Hams Fork (Russell, 1955, p. 8). The spring of 1835 took Russell to the west side of Bear Lake, where he found "about 300 lodges of Snake Indians" (p. 11) and in July of that year he encountered a small party of Shoshone hunting mountain sheep in Jackson Hole (p. 23). The lure of trade still attracted many other Indian groups into the Green River country during and preceding the time of the summer rendezvous. Russell reported an encampment of 400 lodges of Shoshone and Bannock and 100 of Flathead and Nez Percé on the Bear River above the mouth of Smith's Fork on May 9, 1836. The congregation was so large that it was forced to fragment in order to seek subsistence; all planned to return on July 1, when supplies were expected (p. 41). Russell spent the winter of 1840-41 with some 20 lodges of Shoshone in Cache Valley, Utah, and near Great Salt Lake (p. 112).

The general territorial situation had changed little by the end of the fur period. Wislizenus, who visited Wyoming in 1839, commented (1912, p. 76): "In the vicinity [of the Big Horn Mountains] live the Crows....They often rove through the country between the Platte and the Sweet Waters, which are considered by the Indians as a common war ground." Tribes friendly to the Shoshone visited the week-long rendezvous on the Green River. Wislizenus notes that "of the Indians there had come chiefly Snakes, Flatheads, and Nez Percés, peaceful tribes, living beyond the Rocky Mountains" (p. 86).

The journal of Thomas J. Farnham, written in 1839, documents the growing economic difficulties of the Shoshone of the Wyoming-northern Utah area. In July of that year, Farnham received news that the Shoshone on the Bear River were "starving" and subject to the depredations of marauding Blackfoot and Siouan war parties (Farnham, 1906, p. 229). While on "Little Bear River" (a Bear River tributary), Farnham observed that, despite the present barrenness, he had heard that this area was formerly rich in buffalo and that game had abounded in the mountains (p. 233). Further indication of the growing poverty of the Shoshone country is seen in his comment that the Shoshone suffered less from enemy attacks because "the passes through which they enter the Snake country are becoming more and more destitute of game on which to subsist" (pp. 262-263).

Poverty, it would seem, did not bestow complete immunity upon the Shoshone of Wyoming nor did it entirely inhibit occasional forays against their enemies. Father De Smet, who was present at the Green River rendezvous in 1840, wrote that the "Snakes" were then preparing a war party against the Blackfoot (De Smet, 1906, 27:164). But by 1842, the Shoshone had other concerns than the traditionally hostile Blackfoot. Medorem Crawford noted that on July 23, 1842, the encampment of whites then situated near the Sweetwater River was joined by a party of over one hundred "Sues and Shians who had been to fight the Snakes" (Crawford, 1897, p. 13). The Shoshone had experienced previous armed encounters with Siouan groups to the east, but the pressure of the latter in these years was such that the Crow and Shoshone allied for defense against the powerful eastern tribes (Fremont, 1845, p. 146). The Crow, according to Fremont, had been present at the 1842 rendezvous on Green River (p. 50). Despite the alliance, Fremont regarded the Wind River Mountains as the eastern limit of Shoshone occupancy. He noted in 1843 that the Green River was twenty-five years earlier "familiarly known as the Seeds-ke-dee-agai, or Prairie Hen River; a name which it received from the Crows, to whom its upper waters belong" (p. 129), and both Farnham (1906, p. 261) and Russell (1921, pp. 144-146) placed the Shoshone no farther east than the Green River drainage in the years immediately preceding Fremont's observation.

Siouan aggressions continued over an indefinite period, for Bryant reported in June, 1846, that about 3,000 Sioux had collected at Fort Laramie preparatory to an attack against the Shoshone and Crow (Bryant, 1885, p. 107). Bryant and his companions informed the Shoshone of the impending raid when they arrived at Fort Bridger on July 17, 1846. The approximately 500 Shoshone assembled there broke camp immediately, presumably to organize a defense (pp. 142-143).

During the decade of the 1840's, accounts of the presence of Shoshone beyond the Continental Divide are found with increasing frequency. In 1842 W. T. Hamilton, while on the Little Wind River, noted that the trappers and the Shoshone were in continual jeopardy in this region because of "Blackfeet, Bloods, Piegans and Crows" (Hamilton, 1905, p. 52). Although his party was attacked by a Blackfoot group at this time, they sighted a Shoshone party shortly thereafter (p. 61) which was under the leadership of Chief Washakie (pp. 63-64). Other Shoshone joined this group, claiming that they had fought with Pend Oreille Indians near the Owl Creek Mountains on the north side of the Wind River Valley (p. 69). (The identification of this group may well have been erroneous in view of the northerly locale of the Pend Oreille.) The Shoshone met by Hamilton later gathered at Bull Lake to prepare an attack against the Blackfoot on the Big Wind River (p. 71); twenty "Piegans" were later encountered in the Owl Creek Range (p. 80).

These events apparently transpired in the late spring or early summer of 1842, for summer found Washakie's people at Fort Bridger (p. 92), and later at Brown's Hole on the Green River in northwestern Colorado where a "few Ute and Navajos came up on their annual visit with the Shoshone, to trade and to race horses." The Shoshone left for their fall trapping in September (p. 97), but some were there in winter camp when Hamilton's party returned to Brown's Hole to winter (p. 118).

Hamilton's later travels took him on a buffalo hunt into the Big Horn Basin with Washakie in October, 1843 (p. 182). At "Stinking Water" (Shoshone River) the party encountered Crow Indians on their way to visit the Shoshone (p. 183). The buffalo-hunting group returned to the Green River in November for the winter (p. 186). At this time Hamilton noted that Washakie claimed the Big Horn country as far as the Yellowstone River, but that the Crow, Flathead, and Nez Percé hunted upon it and it was regarded as neutral hunting ground by other tribes (p. 187). October, 1848, again found Hamilton in the Big Horn country, where he met a party of Shoshone in the Big Horn Mountains (p. 197). The group was in pursuit of a Cheyenne war party that had stolen horses from them; the offenders were overtaken on the North Platte River and the horses were recovered (p. 198). Hamilton was informed that Washakie was then on Greybull Creek, but planned to move to the Shoshone River (p. 199).

Further information on the activities of the Shoshone east of the Continental Divide comes from Bryant, who, on July 14, 1846, sighted near Green River (Bryant, 1885, p. 136):

> ...a party of some sixty or eighty Shoshone or Snake Indians, who were returning from a buffalo hunt to the east of the South Pass. The chief and active hunters of the party were riding good horses. The others, among whom were some women, were mounted generally upon animals that appeared to have been nearly exhausted by fatigue. These, besides carrying their riders, were freighted with dried buffalo meat, suspended in equal divisions of bulk and weight from straps across the back. Several pack animals were loaded entirely with meat and were driven along as we drive pack mules.

The apparent increase in the use of the Wind River Valley and adjacent areas was in part a result of Crow amity in the face of a common enemy, but it can also be explained in terms of the Shoshone need to seek their winter store of buffalo meat regardless of dangers. The buffalo herds west of the Continental Divide were greatly diminished by 1840, and, by the end of the decade, the intrusion of emigrants must have decimated the remaining stock. As early as 1842, Fremont commented that he saw no buffalo beyond South Pass (Fremont, 1845, p. 63), and in 1849 Major Osborne Cross observed that "scarcely any were to be met with this side of the South Pass" (Cross, 1851, p. 178). The Major later wrote (p. 182):

> Game in this section of the country is scarce, compared with the ranges passed over on the route. We had now gone nearly through the whole buffalo range, as but few are now met with on Bear River. Fifteen years ago they were to be seen in great numbers here, but have been diminishing greatly since that time.

Despite periodic forays to the east, the report of Indian Agent Wilson of Fort Bridger in 1849 indicates that the generally recognized area of Shoshone occupancy was substantially unchanged (J. Wilson, 1849, p. 1002):

> Their claim of boundary is to the east from the Red Buttes [near Casper, Wyoming], on the North Fork of the Platte, to its head in the Park, De-cay-a-que or Buffalo Bull-pen, in the Rocky Mountains; to the south, across the mountains, over to the Yam pa pa, till it enters Green or Colorado River; and then across to the Back bone or ridge of mts. called the Bear River mountains, running nearly due west towards the Salt Lake, so as to take in most of the Salt Lake, and thence on to the Sinks of Mary's or Humboldt River; thence north to the fisheries on the Snake river, in Oregon and thence south (their northern boundary) to the Red Buttes, including the source of Green River.

Joseph Lane, the Superintendent of Indian Affairs in Oregon territory also wrote in that year that "the Shoshonee or Snake Indians inhabit a section of country west of the Rocky mountains, from the summit of these mountains north along Wind river mountains to Henry's fork...." (Lane, 1857, p. 158).

Continuing reference to the presence of Shoshone east of the Continental Divide is found in reports dating from the 1850's, although the Green River country continued as the central area of Eastern Shoshone occupation. Indian Agent Holeman sought to bring the Shoshone to a treaty conference at Fort Laramie in 1851 and reported (Holeman, 1852, p. 445):

...met the village assembled on Sweet Water, about fifty miles east of the South
pass. On the 21st of August I had a talk with them, which resulted in their select-
ing sixty of their headmen, fully authorized to act for the whole tribe....

In September, 1852, Brigham Young arranged a peace conference between the Ute and
Shoshone. The Mormon governor reported (Young, 1852, p. 438):

I then asked the Shoshones how they would like to have us settle upon their lands
at Green River. They replied that the land at Green River did not belong to them;
that they lived and inhabited in the vicinity of the Wind River chain of mountains
and the Sweet River (or Sugar Water, as they called it), but that if we would make
a settlement on Green River they would be glad to come to trade with us.

Difficulties soon developed between the Mormons and the Indians on Green River (Holeman,
1858, pp. 159-160). The report of Lieutenant Fleming of Fort Laramie in 1854 suggests that
the Shoshone had not relinquished the Green River country to the Mormon colonists, despite
Young's claim (H. B. Fleming, 1858, p. 167):

The mountain men have wives and children among the Snake Indians, and therefore claim the right to the Green River country, in virtue of the grant given them
by the Indians, to whom the country belongs, as no treaty has yet been made to
extinguish their title.

The Morehead narrative in Connelley's edition of the Doniphan expedition notes that some
two or three thousand Shoshone were camped on the Green River in the summer of 1857; Chief
Washakie was present at this encampment (Connelley, 1907, p. 607). And Alter's biography of
James Bridger states that in the winter of 1857-58 "Chief Washakie and two thousand Shoshone
tribesmen at the crossing of the Green had no particular difficulty that winter" (Alter, 1925,
p. 303). Forney, in June, 1858, wrote of his plans to establish the Shoshone "under Chief
Wash-A-Kee" on the tributaries of the Green River (Forney, 1860*b*, p. 45) and reported that
the group was located on that river in May, 1858 (Forney, 1859, p. 564).
Albert H. Campbell, General Superintendent of the Pacific Wagon Roads, wrote in 1859 that
the Shoshone were restricted to the area west of the Rockies (1859, p. 8):

The Snakes have received very little attention hitherto from the authorities of the
United States, and frequent wars with their powerful neighbors, the Blackfeet and
Crows, have compelled them in a manner to withdraw from the buffalo range and
keep within the mountain fastnesses, where they derive a scanty subsistence from
roots and the smaller game.

The total context of historical material indicates, however, that the Shoshone were hunting
buffalo on the eastern side of the Continental Divide during this period and, in so doing, were
following a pattern of transmontane hunting familiar to us among the Plateau tribes. Forney
wrote in September, 1858 (1859, p. 564):

I have heretofore spoken of a large tribe of Indians known as the Snakes. They
claim a large tract of country lying in the eastern part of this Territory, but are
scarcely ever found upon their own land.

They generally inhabit the Wind River country, in Oregon and Nebraska Territories, and they sometimes range as far east as Fort Laramie, in the latter Territory.
Their principal subsistence is the buffalo, and it is for the purpose of hunting them
that they range so far east of their own country. This tribe numbers about twelve
hundred souls, all under one principal chief, Wash-a-kee. He has perfect command
over them, and is one of the finest looking and most intellectual Indians I ever saw.

The duration of the previously mentioned peaceful interlude between the Crow and the Shoshone of Wyoming cannot be accurately determined. However, Lander reported them at war in 1858 (1859, p. 49):

> The Crow and Shoshonee Indians having broken out into open war in the north, did not permit of my risking or exposing the large stock of mules of the expedition at the camp selected as the wintering ground of last year's expedition, on Wind River.

Lander encountered Washakie and "the whole of the great tribe of the eastern Shoshonees" hunting antelope on the headwaters of the Green River (p. 68). The Shoshone spent the winter on Wind River but "the last account from them say they are in a starving condition; they are at war with the Crows, and are afraid to go out to hunt for game" (p. 69). The Shoshone had fought with the Crow on October 27, 1858, which had probably prevented them from attempting the fall buffalo hunt. They apparently undertook a hunt during the following spring, for Will H. Wagner, an engineer on the South Pass wagon road, observed in May of 1859 that only a few Shoshone lodges were found on Green River, the main body still being in the Wind River Valley (Wagner, 1861, p. 25).

In February, 1860, Lander wrote a summary of Eastern Shoshone territorial use as of 1859 (1860, pp. 121-122):

> The Eastern Snakes range from the waters of Wind river or latitude 43° 30' on the north and from the South Pass to the headwaters of the North Platte on the east, and to Bear river near the mouth of Smith's Fork on the west. They extend south as far as Brown's Hole on Green River. Their principal subsistence is the roots and seeds of the wild vegetables of the region they inhabit, the mountain trout, with which all the streams of the country are abundantly supplied, and wild game. The latter is now very scarce in the vicinity of the new and old emigrant roads.
>
> The immense herds of antelope I remember having seen along the route of the new road in 1854 and 1857 seem to have disappeared. These Indians visit the border ground between their own country and the Crows and Blackfeet for the purpose of hunting Elk, Antelope and stray herds of buffalo. When these trips are made they travel only in large bands for fear of the Blackfeet and Crows. With the Bannacks and parties of Salt Lake Diggers they often make still longer marches into the northwestern buffalo ranges on the head waters of the Missouri and Yellow Stone.
>
> These excursions usually last over winter, the more western Indians who join them passing over a distance of twelve hundred miles on the out and return journey.

Under the leadership of Washakie, which dates from approximately the beginning of the period of heavy emigration to the Far West, the Shoshone of Wyoming had maintained amicable relations with the whites. The early 1860's, however, saw increased clashes between Indians and whites in the Bear River country and in southern Idaho. While the activities of Chief Pocatello's band and of other hostile groups will be further discussed in the section on Idaho, it would be well at this point to clarify relations between Washakie's followers and the people of Bear River. It is impossible to differentiate a Wyoming group as distinct from the Shoshone of Bear River in earlier periods, and, in view of the presence of buffalo in the country of the Green and Bear rivers until at least 1840, it is more than probable that southwestern Wyoming, northern Utah, and southeastern Idaho were common grounds roamed over by several nomadic hunting groups. Lander recognized the affinity between the areas, although he distinguished Washakie's Eastern Shoshone from the Utah residents on the basis of their respective relations with the whites (Lander, 1860, pp. 122-123):

The Salt Lake Diggers intermarry with the Eastern Snakes and are on good terms
with them.

Among these Indians [the "Salt Lake Diggers"] are some of the worst in the mountains. Washakie will not permit a horse thief or vagabond to remain in his band,
but many of the Mormon Indians go about the country with minor chiefs calling
themselves Eastern Snakes.

Old Snag, a chief sometimes seen on Green River, who proclaims himself an Eastern Snake, and friend of the Americans, is of this class....

Southern Indians pass, on their way "to buffalo," (a technical term,) through the
lands of the Eastern Snakes and Bannocks, and the latter are often made to bear
the blame of their horse-stealing proclivities.

Doty reported depredations on the road between Fort Laramie and Salt Lake City in 1862
(Doty, 1863, pp. 342, 355), and in the following year the Army attacked a large number of the
hostiles on Bear River and inflicted very severe losses on them (War of the Rebellion, 1902, pp.
185-187). Doty reported from Box Elder, Utah, on July 30 of the same year (ibid., p. 219):

A treaty of peace was this day concluded at this place by Gen. Connor [who led the
Bear River attack] and myself with the bands of the Shoshones, of which Pocatello,
San Pitch and Sagwich are the principal chiefs.

Earlier, on July 2, 1863, a treaty was entered into at Fort Bridger between Doty and the
bands of "Waushakee," "Shauwuno," "Tibagan," "Peoastoagah," "Totimee," "Ashingodimah,"
"Sagowitz," "Oretzimawik," "Bazil," and "Sanpitz" (Doty, 1865, p. 319). Doty noted at this
time that the Shoshone "claim their ... eastern boundary on the crest of the Rocky mountains;
but it is certain that they, as well as the Bannacks, hunt buffalo below the Three Forks of the
Missouri, and on the headwaters of the Yellowstone" (p. 318). Doty continued (pp. 318-319):

As none of the Indians of this country have permanent places of abode, in their
hunting excursions they wander over an immense region, extending from the fisheries at and below Salmon Falls, on the Shoshone [Snake] river, near the Oregon
line, to the sources of that stream and to the Buffalo country beyond....

The Shoshonees and Bannocks are the only nations which, to my knowledge hunt
together over the same ground.

The Shoshone continued to hunt beyond the mountains after the Fort Bridger treaty. Superintendent Irish reported in September, 1864, that the "Shoshonees" were at Bear Lake await-
ing their payment and were impatient to "go to their winter hunting grounds on Wind River"
(Irish, 1865, p. 314). Three hundred Cheyenne lodges were reported in Wind River Valley in
May, 1865, but the group subsequently withdrew to the "Sweetwater mountains and thence to
Powder River" (Coutant, 1899, 1:440). In September, 1865, Irish reported that the Shoshone
frequented the Wind River country and the headwaters of the North Platte and Missouri rivers
(Irish, 1866, p. 311). The Superintendent described the pattern of movement that had become
established (ibid.):

Their principal subsistence is the buffalo, which they hunt during the fall, winter,
and spring, on which they subsist during that time, and return in the summer to
Fort Bridger and Great Salt Lake City.

Agent Luther Mann of Fort Bridger added (1865, p. 327):

They spend about eight months of the year among the Wind River mountains and in the valley of the Wind River, Big Horn and Yellowstone....

The Shoshonees are friendly with the Bannacks, their neighbor on the north ...but are hostile toward the tribes on their eastern boundaries, viz: Sioux, Arapahoes, Cheyennes, and Crows.

Mann observed that the Eastern Shoshone numbered some 150 lodges. However, he also noted that Washakie claimed to be too weak to fight his enemies. In his next year's report, Mann wrote that on September 20, 1865, the Shoshone set out from Fort Bridger for the Wind River and Popo Agie valleys where they hunted buffalo, deer, elk, and mountain sheep and passed the winter. Only five to ten lodges remained on Green River for the winter (ibid., p. 126).

The Shoshone had some difficulty with hostile tribes during their hunts in the Wind River Valley. The battle of Crowheart Butte (near Crowheart, Wyoming) has become a legend on the Wind River Reservation, and the facts of the event have become well embellished. More reliable informants claim that the Crow were encamped at the present site of Kinnear, Wyoming, on the north side of Big Wind River and were driven out after a strong attack by the Shoshone. The Crow detachment was evidently not merely a war party, for the men were accompanied by their women and children. Hebard, using documentary material unavailable to the writers, places the date of this battle as March, 1866 (Hebard, 1930, p. 151). There is no further mention in the sources of Crow occupation of the Wind River Valley.

This was not the end of the Shoshones' troubles, however, for in the following year (1867), Indian Agent Mann noted (1868, p. 182):

> Immediately after the distribution of their annuity goods last year, they left this agency for their hunting grounds in the Popeaugie [Popo Agie River, near Lander, Wyo.] and Wind River valleys, the only portion of the country claimed by them where they can obtain buffalo.

> Early last spring the near approach of hostile Sioux and Cheyennes compelled them to leave before they could prepare their usual supply of dried meat for summer use.

Mann further reported that, after being paid the annuity on June 8, 1867, "they have since gone to the valley of the Great Salt Lake, as is usual with them, preparatory to their return to their hunting grounds in autumn" (p. 183). These accounts further document the manner in which the Utah and Wyoming populations merged.

The Sioux were apparently especially active east of the Wind River Range in these years and many other attacks were reported. The Shoshone went to Wind River in 1868 and were again attacked by the Sioux. Agent Mann reported that year that a few small bands of Shoshone had not hunted buffalo in two years for fear of attack (Mann, 1869, pp. 616-618).

The government had a good deal of difficulty in persuading the Shoshone to remain on the reservation established by the treaty of 1868. Captain J. H. Patterson, the new agent, wrote in 1869 (1870, p. 717): "So powerful are the Sioux, it is only after winter is far advanced, and from that time until early in the spring, that the Shoshones can remain on the reservation." They passed the winter of 1868-69 at Wind River, but the Sioux attacked on April 26, 1869, before they broke winter camp (J. A. Campbell, 1870, p. 173). On September 14, 1869, Siouan warriors attempted another foray into Wind River Valley but were repulsed by troops. Fearful of another early attack and wary of their new reservation co-residents, the Northern Arapaho and Washakie left Wind River at the end of April of the following year (1870). The Shoshone departed with little stored meat, since they were unable to pursue the buffalo far out on the prairie (G. W. Fleming, 1871, p. 643).

In the following years, we hear little of the hunting activities of the Shoshone. They were moved permanently to the Wind River Reservation, where, according to Agent James Irwin in 1873, they showed a strong desire to abandon their nomadic ways and to learn agriculture

(Irwin, 1874, p. 612). Irwin claimed that, although the Bannock population of the "Shoshone and Bannock Agency" at Wind River was transferred in 1872 to Fort Hall, 216 still unsettled Shoshone had expressed intent in the following year to move to Wind River. The Shoshone experienced little success in their early attempts at farming, and the government food allotments were seldom adequate to last through the year. This, combined with the traditional value placed on the buffalo hunt, perpetuated the nomadic pattern for a number of years. As late as 1877, Agent Patten wrote (1878, p. 605):

> During the month of October last [1876], while the Shoshones were on one of their annual hunts, the village became divided; Washakie, with the greater portion, struck across the country from the base of the Sierra Shoshone Mountains to the mouth of Owl Creek on Big Wind River; the smallest party, under two braves named Na-akie and Ta-goon-dum, started for the river above the mouth of Grey Bull, where having arrived the prospect of a successful hunt was propitious. Large herds of buffalo were everywhere in sight; but the next morning after their arrival this little band, comprising men, women, and children, were suddenly attacked by Dull Knife's band of hostile Cheyenne warriors.

The Plains were evidently still unsafe, and hunting parties traveled in strength. But the end of the buffalo period was not far off, for hide-hunters and settlers had already made massive inroads on the herds, and the open-range cattle-raising industry had begun. It is interesting to note, however, that the itinerary followed in 1876 was much the same as that related by Shimkin's informants and by ours. Except for that given in the one account by Hamilton, it has no antecedents in the historical literature.

EARLY RESERVATION PERIOD

Wind River Shoshone informants speak little of activities west of the Continental Divide and tend to place their early economic life almost entirely in the Missouri drainage. This is not surprising when it is considered that eighty-six years had passed between the signing of the Fort Bridger treaty of July 3, 1868, establishing the reservation, and the field work reported here. Almost seventy years had elapsed between that date and Shimkin's 1937-1938 field work. That informants have a one-dimensional view of earlier periods in Shoshone history may well be expected. The type of data that deals with locales and events, the movements of peoples and situational adaptation is history of a different kind from the traditional cultural material with which anthropologists usually work. It would be an understatement to say that it would tax the memory of any human being to ask exactly where and when his people hunted many years before he was born. One of the oldest living Shoshone, for example, responded to our question about the location of the chief's lodge in the camp by saying that the chiefs lived in log cabins near the Agency. And even this was quite a mnemonic feat.

Most of the following data was obtained from informants and pertains primarily to the early reservation period. Even for such a relatively late time, the information is not wholly reliable and is often vague and fragmentary. Certain aspects of these data are perpetuated in Wind River tradition, however, and are valid for even earlier periods than the one discussed. These concern the yearly economic cycle, the rhythm of movement from buffalo prairies to the mountains, the coalescence and fragmentation of social groups, the types of fish and game taken and the technology involved-cultural facts not immediately linked to situational, historical factors. These comments on reliability of informants' data should be borne in mind throughout the account below.

The stable center of Eastern Shoshone settlement pattern was the winter camp. All informants agreed that the chief winter camps were in the valleys of the Big and Little Wind rivers, in the region of the present Diversion Dam and Fort Washakie, respectively. There they were protected from winter storms, and the winds blew enough snow from the ground to allow the horses to graze. In the bottomlands by the streams they found water and firewood and enjoyed the protection of the cottonwood trees. In the period before the ending of intertribal hostilities in Wyoming camps were closely clustered to allow for mutual defense in the event of an attack, but after the pacification of the area, people pitched their tipis farther apart. Although never safe from attack, the Shoshone had greater security during the winter, since the cold and snows made their enemies relatively immobile also.

Winter residence at Wind River was not obligatory. Smaller groups were said to camp on the western slope of the Wind River Mountains, in the vicinity of Pinedale, and others remained near Fort Bridger. Contemporary informants gave no confirmation of Shimkin's statement that a group of Shoshone, under Washakie, customarily wintered in the Absaroka Mountain foothills on the head of the Grey Bull River (Shimkin, 1947a, p. 247). Also, Shimkin's chart, which shows that Shoshone occasionally spent the winter in the Powder and Sweetwater River valleys (p. 279), probably indicates the true situation only for the period after the area became secure from attack, in the 1870's. All of these locales would be highly vulnerable to hostiles, as was the Wind River Valley in the pre-reservation era, and it is highly probable that Shimkin's informants spoke of post-reservation events and not of a traditional pattern.

Subsistence during the winter was gained chiefly from the stored yield of the fall buffalo hunt. The meat was dried and pounded and placed in large rawhide bags. True pemmican was not manufactured, although the pulverized buffalo meat was mixed with dried roots and berries preparatory to being eaten.

Stores frequently ran low towards the end of winter, and some hardship resulted. However, the stored food was supplemented by elk which had been driven out of the mountains by snow, and by antelope and deer meat. Rabbits were also snared.

Some informants stated that the Shoshone went into winter camp as early as October. Others, however, reported that the winter camp was made as late as December. It would seem that November to December are the more probable times. Support for this date is found in Shimkin (1947a, p. 279).

The winter camp broke up in February or March, and the spring buffalo hunt was then launched. This was a collective venture, as opposed to the sporadic and individual hunting that went on during the winter. Informants were extremely vague in saying whether all the winter camp went on the spring hunt together or whether they broke up into parties. Shimkin states that the Shoshone split into four bands when buffalo hunting (p. 247). Some of my own informants, however, said that all hunted in one group under Washakie. Others said that there were several chiefs, and each took his people where he chose.

The buffalo in springtime were not of good quality, and the lean, tough meat was considered very inferior to the fat meat obtained in the fall. Informants said that the chief purpose of the spring hunt was to obtain hides for tipis (and all the other uses to which buffalo hide was put) and to get fresh meat. The spring hunt was generally pursued in the Big Horn Basin, although there were buffalo in the Wind River Valley itself, which were also hunted. Although the former locale is most frequently mentioned, it should be assumed that the migratory habits of the buffalo imposed some variability.

After the spring hunt, the Shoshone reconvened in Wind River Valley and in June held their Sun Dance. This was a period of general gathering and involved visits of people from other areas.

After the Sun Dance was concluded, the participants withdrew from the valley lands and retired to the Green River country and the mountains until the autumn buffalo hunt. At this time, the larger buffalo-hunt and Sun Dance group broke into small units and scattered in several directions. Shimkin maps some of the trails followed by the summer hunting parties (p. 249). Although there was considerable deviation from the trails he indicates, they show a penetration of the Yellowstone and Jackson Hole country, the Owl Creek Mountains, and the Green River and Bear River regions.

Shimkin's chart of the yearly subsistence cycle shows June and July as a period of intertribal rendezvous while August and early September were spent in family groups (p. 279). My informants indicated that small groups of families were the essential social and economic units from June to September; the trade rendezvous held in the Green River country ended by 1840. Some Shoshone said the summer group consisted of only one tipi, while others claimed that this was a post-reservation pattern. In earlier times, it was said, the need for security from attack caused groups of from six to ten tipis (this figure is highly uncertain) to travel together. These summer groups were probably the most stable and cohesive units in Eastern Shoshone society, although there was a good deal of interchange of members.

Although each summer group often followed the same general route every year, other groups could and did hunt this territory. There was no sense of group or band ownership of the lands habitually visited, and a group could alter or change its route. In June many people went to the Sweetwater region and across South Pass to hunt antelope. Antelope were also hunted at various times of the year north of Wind River on the benches at the foot of the Owl Creek Range and in the Green River country. In the latter area, the Eastern Shoshone were frequently joined in September by Shoshone and Bannock from Idaho.

There were several routes to the Jackson Hole and Yellowstone country. The Yellowstone does not seem to have been visited as frequently before the final pacification of the area, owing, no doubt, to the proximity of Crow and Blackfoot. Some groups followed the most direct route-through the Wind River Valley and across Togwatee Pass (the present route of U. S. Highway 287). Others hunted first in the Owl Creek Mountains and then crossed west into the Wind River Valley at Dubois and thence through Togwatee Pass. Still another route led through the "Rough Trail," now called Washakie Pass, in the Wind River Range and gave access to the Pinedale area and the western slope of the range. From that point, groups hunted in this immediate region or went northwest to Jackson Hole or south to the Fort Bridger area. Any one of these routes could be used for the return to Wind River and the subsequent fall buffalo hunt, but there was a tendency to return by a different trail than that used on the outward trip.

Summer subsistence activities were varied, but none called for extensive coöperation beyond the immediate family or the small summer group. Antelope hunting west of the Continental Divide called for some joint endeavor, though not on the scale of the buffalo hunt. Moose and elk were hunted by smaller parties in the high mountain parks and forests of the Wind River, Grand Teton, and Owl Creek Mountains. The last range was especially noted for a plentiful supply of mountain sheep. Deer were killed and rabbits were taken throughout the year. Sage hens were snared in the spring, and duck were killed on Bull Lake in Wind River Valley in the fall. After 1840, there were almost no buffalo left on the west side of the Wind River Range, although before that time they were pursued there by the Shoshone. However, the Wind River Valley abounded in buffalo until relatively late, for the worst excesses of the white hide-hunters did not begin until after the Civil War. Buffalo were also killed in the Owl Creek and Wind River foothills and were taken also in Jackson Hole and Yellowstone Park. Also, a smaller variety of buffalo, called timber buffalo, which did not follow the migratory pattern of the larger Plains type, was killed in the high mountain parks.

Fish were of fundamental importance, especially, according to Shimkin (1947*a*, p. 268), during the spring. Mountain trout were the main fish; the Eastern Shoshone did not join their colinguists in salmon fishing on the Columbia waters, at least during this later period. Shimkin specifically states that "no private ownership of good fishing places existed, and dams and weirs were not maintained from year to year" (ibid.). This accords with our own field data.

Summer economic activities involved little estensive coöperation and, since game was scattered through the mountains rather than concentrated in large herds, the small groups of families were the most effective economic units. It is significant in this connection that, as soon as the security of the country was guaranteed by the presence of the whites, the one-or two-tipi summer camp displaced its somewhat larger predecessor. Game in the pre-treaty period was plentiful in the Wyoming mountains and a single family or small group of tipis could gain adequate subsistence; the principal reason for larger gatherings in the summer was defense. The yield probably became better after camp groups became smaller, for locales were not hunted out as rapidly.

The only economic activity other than the buffalo hunt which called for the coöperation of a large group of men was antelope hunting. Antelope were usually surrounded by the hunters and run in circles by relays of mounted men. Unlike the Nevada population, the Eastern Shoshone did not build brush corrals or employ antelope shamans.

Women's economic life could be pursued by individuals. In addition to cooking, dressing skins, and other household chores, women's efforts provided all the vegetable foods consumed by the Shoshone. This activity went on from summer into fall. Various berries were collected; gooseberries, currants, buffalo berries, and chokecherries being the most important. All these berries grew near streams and ripened about August. Gooseberries and chokecherries can be found in the mountains and foothills while buffalo berries and currants grow in the lower valleys. The berries were dried and stored for future use.

Roots, also, were a valuable adjunct to the diet. Yamp, the principal root, was found in the mountains. Bitterroot was dug on prairie hills, wild potatoes were found in the foothills, and the wild onion grew in the valley floors. Although special trips were not made to root grounds (in contrast to the congregations for camas in Idaho) the women dug them out with pointed sticks near favorable hunting camps. One informant spoke, for example, of the rich yamp grounds in the Big Horn Mountains. All the women of the camp group went out together to dig roots. This was for purposes of companionship; each woman dug and kept her own tubers.

In September, the scattered camp groups reunited at Wind River for the fall buffalo hunt. The buffalo was a critical factor in Wind River subsistence, for it provided the margin of survival through the long winter. The Eastern Shoshone were frequently joined in the buffalo hunt by other Shoshone from the Bear River country and, less often, by Shoshone and Bannock from

Idaho. The last two groups usually hunted buffalo in Montana with certain Plateau tribes, and their routes did not usually coincide. Informants uniformly said that all the Eastern Shoshone went out to hunt buffalo together, and Shimkin (1947a, p. 280) states that "in full strength, often with Bannocks or others accompanying them, they would cross the Wind River Range" for the fall hunt. It seems certain that, insofar as they may have penetrated far north into the Big Horn Basin, numerical strength was necessary during the immediate pre-reservation period and shortly thereafter.

As the buffalo camp moved out on the range, scouts were sent ahead to locate the herds. The actual techniques used by hunters were much the same as among the Plains tribes. Ideally, two horses were used, one for riding within reach of the herd, the other a swift horse trained to run close to the buffalo while avoiding the animal's horns. The herd was surrounded and run, and the flanking hunters shot arrows and launched spears at the prey. When a buffalo was killed, the hunter threw an arrow or some personal, identifying possession on the carcass to mark it as his.

This was apparently the main technique for buffalo hunting. They were not stampeded over cliffs, as was the practice of some Indian tribes. One informant said that Chief Washakie would not permit it for reasons of conservation. Occasionally, hunters on foot stalked and killed buffalo with the bow and arrow, but such activities did not take place during the communal hunts.

When on the fall hunt, individual hunters did not attack the herds, for the animals might stampede for long distances after only one or two were killed. The fall hunt was organized coöperatively, but informants denied the existence of the typical Plains police, or soldier, societies or any comparable form of institutionalized discipline to prevent individual hunting.

The time spent in the fall hunt, including travel, appears to have been about two months-from mid-September to mid-November. Meat and hides were prepared by the women and packed back to winter camp. Shimkin doubts the efficiency of the buffalo hunt (1947a, p. 266). If it is assumed that each family had from five to ten horses, three of which were needed to drag the tipi and utensil-loaded travois and three for riding, only two horses were, according to his reasoning, available for packing. Since one would be loaded with hides for trade, only one was available for carrying meat. The supply carried was sufficient for no more than twenty days, Shimkin concludes.

The mounted buffalo hunters were not the only Shoshone inhabitants of Wyoming, and one more group remains to be discussed. In the mountain chain extending from the Wind River Range northwest to the Teton and Gros Ventres ranges and northward into Yellowstone lived a Shoshone population known as the Dukarika, or Sheepeaters. These Dukarika are not to be confused with a Shoshone population of the same name in the mountains of Idaho. The two were socially and geographically separate; their common name is due only to the fact that there were mountain sheep in the habitats of both. The name thus has no more significance in terms of political organization than do the food names applied to Shoshone living in certain areas of Nevada and Idaho.

There is little documentary information on the Dukarika, and contemporary Wind River informants knew very little about them. Our earliest reference to these secluded people is found in Bonneville's journals, when, in September, 1833, three Indians were sighted in the Wind River Range. Irving writes (1850, p. 139):

> Captain Bonneville at once concluded that these belonged to a kind of hermit race, scanty in number, that inhabit the highest and most inaccessible fastnesses. They speak the Shoshone language and probably are offsets from that tribe, though they have peculiarities of their own, which distinguish them from all other Indians. They are miserably poor, own no horses, and are destitute of every convenience to be derived from an intercourse with the whites. Their weapons are bows and stone-pointed arrows, with which they hunt the deer, the elk, and the mountain sheep. They are to be found scattered about the countries of the Shoshone, Flathead, Crow, and Blackfeet tribes; but their residences are always in lonely places, and the clefts of rocks.

Osborne Russell, when trapping in Lamar Valley in Yellowstone Park in July, 1835, observed (1955, p. 26):

> Here we found a few Snake Indians comprising six men, seven women, and eight or ten children who were the only inhabitants of this lonely and secluded spot. They were all neatly clothed in dressed deer and sheep skins of the best quality and seemed to be perfectly contented and happy.

The Indians had "about thirty dogs on which they carried their skins, clothing, provisions, etc., on their hunting excursions. They were well armed with bows and arrows pointed with obsidian" (ibid.). Russell also saw other "Mountain Snakes" near the headwaters of the Shoshone River (ibid., p. 64). Speaking of the Dukarika, Hiram Chittenden says (1933, p. 8):

> It was a humble branch of the Shoshone family which alone is known to have dwelt in the region of Yellowstone Park. They were called Tuakuarika, or more commonly Sheepeaters. They were found in the park country at the time of its discovery, and had doubtless long been there. The Indians were veritable hermits of the mountains, utterly unfit for warlike contention, and seem to have sought immunity from their dangerous neighbors by dwelling among the inaccessible fastnesses of the mountains.

Chittenden continues:

> We-Saw [an Indian who accompanied Capt. Jones in 1873] states that he had neither knowledge nor tradition of any permanent occupants of the Park save the timid Sheepeaters....He said that his people [Shoshone], the Bannocks, and the Crows, occasionally visited the Yellowstone Lake and River.

Captain W. A. Jones, when on his 1873 expedition to Yellowstone Park, commented that one of the Indians with him, a Sheepeater, knew the route back to Wind River (Jones, 1875, p. 39). Beyond these few citations, the Sheepeaters are almost unmentioned.

In contrast to the previously described Shoshone, the Dukarika traveled mostly on foot, although a very few had horses. They hunted timber buffalo near the mountain lakes and killed elk, deer, and the mountain sheep for which they were named. Antelope were occasionally hunted near Pinedale by those who owned horses. The best hunting grounds were considered to be those near Pinedale and on the west slope of the Wind River Range. Although some Sheepeaters inhabited Yellowstone Park, their main hunting grounds were farther south. The Sheepeaters were by no means the only Indians who made use of the Yellowstone region. Hultkrantz also mentions entry by parties of "Kiowa, Plains Shoshoni, Lemhi Shoshoni, Bannock, Crow, Blackfoot and Nez Percé" (Hultkrantz, 1954, p. 140).

All game was tracked and cornered by dogs and dispatched with the bow and arrow; the buffalo lance was used only by mounted hunters of Plains buffalo. Dogs were also used for packing-both on back and by travois.

In addition to their hunting activities, the Sheepeaters speared trout in the spring and summer. Nets, traps, and weirs were apparently not used. They also made use of the wild vegetables (previously listed) that grow in the mountains.

The Sheepeaters stayed in the mountains during the winter and did not join the valley winter camps of the buffalo hunters. They lived on stored meat and also continued to take elk, rabbits, and deer. Hunting was usually done on snowshoes.

Their camp groups were small, and, although no exact figure could be obtained, they never numbered more than the occupants of a few buffalo-hide tipis. Each such group had its leader who decided the hunting itinerary. The Dukarikas had no over-all political organization; each small camp group was politically and economically autonomous. "Dukarika," then, can be assumed to be a term defining a type of economic adaptation rather than a social unit.

The discreet Dukarika social units did not assert hunting rights to particular territories. Any group could hunt where it pleased, and they in no way resisted or resented the entry of the mounted Shoshone during the summer. Although they undoubtedly had contact with the latter, they did not join the spring or fall buffalo hunts, nor did they at any time during the pre-treaty period acknowledge the political leadership of the valley people. After the reservation was established, however, they left the mountains and settled in the Trout Creek section of the Wind River Reservation.

EASTERN SHOSHONE TERRITORY

Thus far, we have presented the pertinent historical data on Shoshone ecology in Wyoming and adjacent parts of northern Utah and we have described the annual cycle of economic activities during the early reservation period. The following summary of information on Eastern Shoshone territory will consider both kinds of data but will not attempt to delineate the social and political affiliations of the peoples using the lands. This subject, as the previously cited statement by Shimkin suggests (p. 300), is extremely complex and will be reserved for further discussion.

The most perplexing problem presented by the Eastern Shoshone is the extent of their penetration into the Missouri River waters. Although the Shoshone evidently undertook forays at least as far east as Fort Laramie, contemporary informants and historical sources agree that their main hunting grounds extended no farther east than the Sweetwater and other headwaters of the North Platte River. We have no certain information of Shoshone use of lands east of the upper Sweetwater River, and informants gave no data on this sector.

Wind River Shoshone informants relate the itineraries of buffalo-hunting parties northward into the Big Horn Basin. The fall and spring buffalo hunts were said to have taken place in the region of Thermopolis, Wyoming, and as far north as Cody and Greybull, Wyoming. The region east of the Big Horn Mountains was thought by informants to have been occasionally visited, but was acknowledged as the hunting grounds of hostile tribes. The presence of a "mixed party of Shoshone and Flatheads" in the Big Horn Mountains was noted by the westward-bound Astoria party in 1811 (Irving, 1890, p. 196) and indicates some early penetration of the area, although the presence of Flathead Indians suggests that the party had entered the area via Idaho and Montana and not from Green River. However, pre-reservation historical data show that before the 1840's the Eastern Shoshone largely restricted their buffalo hunting to the region west of the Continental Divide and sporadically penetrated the Wind River and Big Horn basins only after the buffalo disappeared from the country beyond the Rockies. Their entry into the eastern buffalo range became more frequent in the 1850's, but it by no means constituted an exclusive monopoly on lands there. They depended upon their numbers for protection and were forced to compete with other tribes for the right to hunt on the land. Their hunting excursions were in the nature of forays and were unsuccessful in some years. They enjoyed security and some assurance of success in the hunt only after they had been placed under the protection of Federal troops and the Crow had been placed on reservations. That the center of Shoshone occupancy lay west of the Continental Divide was affirmed by Chief Washakie. Agent Head wrote in 1867 (1868, p. 186):

> Washakee said that the country east from the Wind river mountains, to the settled portions of eastern Nebraska and Kansas, had always been claimed by four principal Indian tribes-the Sioux, Arapahoes, Cheyennes, and Crows.

Further evidence that the valleys of the Big Horn and Wind rivers were used only for buffalo hunting and not stably occupied in the pre-reservation period is indicated by the Shoshones' ignorance of the hunting grounds in the surrounding mountains. Captain Jones used Shoshone guides from Camp Brown on the new Wind River Reservation when he undertook his exploration of Yellowstone Park in 1873. The captain and his party penetrated the Owl Creek Range, north of the reservation and found at the head of Owl Creek a lovely park (Jones, 1875, p. 54):

> This park bears many evidences of having been used as a hiding place. Our Indians knew nothing of it, and yet there are all through it numerous trails, old lodge poles, bleached bones of game, and old camps of Cheyennes and Arapahoes.

Shimkin (1947*a*, p. 248) notes that this park was one of the "foci" of Shoshone nomadic activity, a place to which Wind River people repaired for summer hunting. Although this is true for later times, it certainly was not so in the pre-reservation period when hunts on the Missouri waters were conducted only for limited periods and in the plains and valleys where buffalo were to be found.

Until the late 1860's the Wind River Valley and the Big Horn Basin and Mountains were zones of penetration rather than occupation of the Eastern Shoshone. Another such zone is in the Tetons and Yellowstone. This is confirmed by the journal of Captain Jones, who commented upon the unfamiliarity of his Shoshone guides with the country around Yellowstone Lake (Jones, 1875, p. 23). He wrote (p. 34):

> ... the Indians have failed to find the trail back to Yellowstone Lake.... The explanation of this is that they are "Plains Indians," and are wholly unaccustomed to travel among forests like these.

Later, the exploring party reached the upper Yellowstone River, above the lake, where Jones commented (p. 39):

> We have now reached a country from which one of our Indians says he knows the way back to Camp Brown by the head of Wind River. He belongs to a band of Shoshones called "Sheepeaters," who have been forced to live for a number of years in the mountains away from the tribe.

The Yellowstone area was frequently entered by the Crow and was evidently not a Shoshone hunting territory, except for the Sheepeaters. Jackson Hole is more commonly mentioned by informants as a place of summer hunting activity, but the above information from Jones would suggest that parties entered it from the Green River country rather than from Wind River. The Eastern Shoshone apparently did not move west of the Tetons except when visiting the Shoshone and Bannock of Idaho. It should be mentioned at this point that the Shoshone and Bannock also hunted in the Jackson Hole and Yellowstone country, probably to a greater extent than did the Eastern Shoshone, and the frequent mention of parties of Blackfoot and other hostiles in the country both east and west of the Teton Range indicates that the weaker Shoshone experienced no little danger there.

The valley of the Salt River in western Wyoming was used by both Idaho and Wyoming Shoshone. Idaho Shoshone and Bannock frequently entered the valleys of the Green River and its tributaries to hunt antelope in the fall. These people apparently mixed so frequently with the Eastern Shoshone in this area that it is most expedient to differentiate the respective populations according to where they wintered. On the west, Wind River Shoshone informants now make little mention of any use of the Bear River and Bear Lake country, despite the apparent interchangeability of population in the pre-reservation period; again, it must be assumed that informant data does not much antedate the move to Wind River.

The southern and southeastern limits of the Shoshone range in Wyoming are most vague. They probably extended as far south as the Yampa River in Colorado and the Uinta Range in Utah; Lander places their southern limits at Brown's Hole, in northwestern Colorado on the Green River (Lander, 1860, p. 121).

It is doubtful whether the country as far east as the North Platte and south to the Yampa was intensively exploited. Informants knew of no significant activities which went on in those areas, although they thought that antelope were occasionally hunted there. Most agreed that the Sweetwater River and Rawlins, Wyoming, were in Shoshone country, but Casper, Wyoming, and the Medicine Bow Mountains were excluded. Shimkin's map shows no regular utilization of the southeastern corner of Shoshone country (Shimkin, 1947a, map 1, p. 249), although my informants spoke of antelope hunts on the south side of South Pass. We can conclude that this whole area was, like many other sections, an area of occasional penetration. It is doubtful whether the poorly watered country between the Green and North Platte rivers was intensively used by any Indian group.

SOCIAL AND POLITICAL ORGANIZATION

A good deal of Eastern Shoshone social organization has already been described in the section on the subsistence cycle and in the context of historical data. Although the summer was spent in scattered groups, the collective buffalo hunt and the large winter camp made these Shoshone among the best organized of all the Shoshone population. Horses, a richer game supply, and the constant need for protection caused the Eastern Shoshone to travel in much larger groups than those of Nevada and perhaps also of Idaho, and leadership was, correspondingly, more highly developed. We hear early of the " 'Horn Chief,' a distinguished chief and warrier of the Shoshonee tribe," who was frequently encountered in the Bear River region (Ferris, 1940, pp. 71-73). Ferris also tells of two other Shoshone chiefs, but does not localize them or their following (p. 309):

> The principal chief of the Snakes is called the *"Iron Wristband,"* a deceitful fellow, who pretends to be a great friend of the whites, and promises to punish his followers for killing them or stealing their horses. The *"Little Chief"* a brave young warrior, is the most noble and honorable character among them.

Ferris also mentions a Shoshone leader named "Cut Nose," who, he said, assumed white dress and left the tribe (p. 310).

During the 1840's the name of Washakie is mentioned with increasing frequency in historical sources and thereafter this chief overshadows all other leaders. We first hear of him from the trapper Russell who recorded a conversation at Weber River, Utah, in which the Shoshone leaders were discussed (Russell, 1921, pp. 114-116).

> One remarked that the Snake chief, Pah-da-hewak um da was becoming very unpopular and it was the opinion of the Snakes in general that Moh-woom-hah, his brother, would be at the head of affairs before twelve months, as his village already amounted to more than three hundred lodges, and, moreover, he was supported by the bravest men in the nation, among whom were Ink-a-tosh-a-pop, Fibe-bo-un-to-wat-see and Who-sha-kik, who were the pillars of the nation and at whose names the Blackfeet quaked with fear.

The death of the first two brothers in 1842 and 1843 resulted in considerable disorganization, according to Russell, and "the tribe scattered in smaller villages over the country in consequence of having no chief who could control and keep them together" (pp. 145-146).

Washakie is next mentioned in Hamilton's journal as a Shoshone chief encountered on Wind River (Hamilton, 1905, p. 63). In 1849, Agent Wilson listed him among the chiefs of the mounted Shoshone (J. Wilson, 1849, p. 1002).

> The principal chiefs of the Sho-sho-nies are Mono, about forty-five years old, so called from a wound in the face or cheek, from a ball that disfigures him; Wiskin, Cut-hair; Washikick, Gourd-rattle, (with whom I have had an interview;) and Oapichi, Big Man. Of the Sho-sho-nees Augatsira is the most noted.

Washakie maintained good relations with the whites and in 1852 appeared in Salt Lake City to arrange peaceful trade with the Mormons. Also in 1852, Brigham Young's peace conference between the Ute and Shoshone included "Anker-howhitch (Arrow-pine being sick) and thirty-four lodges; on the part of the Shoshones, Wah-sho-kig, To-ter-mitch, Watchenamp, Ter-ret-e-ma, Pershe-go, and twenty-six lodges...." (Young, 1852, p. 437). Of these five Shoshone chiefs, only Washakie is subsequently mentioned in the literature. Brigham Young apparently recognized Washakie as the leader of the Eastern Shoshone, for in or about 1854 he sent a Mormon, Bill Hickman, to establish contact with Washakie in the Green River country (Hickman, 1872, p. 105). Superintendent Forney reported of the Shoshone in 1859 (1860*a*, p. 731):

> One of these [the fourteen bands listed by Forney], by common consent, is denom-
> inated a tribe, and is under the complete control of Chief Was-a-kee, assisted by
> four to six sub-chiefs. These number, at least, twelve hundred.

If this census is accurate, this number must have included most of the Eastern Shoshone population.

Washakie gained fame as the friend of the white man. This reputation was well deserved, for the wagon route through southwestern Wyoming was made quite safe for the emigrants through his efforts. Furthermore, hostile, predatory bands never developed among the Eastern Shoshone as they did among the Shoshone and Paiute to the west. In a report dated February, 1860, Lander observed (1860, p. 121): "No instance is on record of the Eastern Snakes having committed outrages upon the whites." We obtain a fuller description of Washakie in the same report (p. 122).

> Wash-ikeek, the principal Chief of the tribe, is half Flathead. He obtained his
> popularity in the nation by various feats as a warrior and, it is urged by some of the
> mountaineers, by his extreme severity. This has, in one or two instances, extended
> so far as taking life. The word Washikee or Washikiek signifies "Gambler's Gourd."
> He was originally called "Pina-qua-na" or "Smell of Sugar." "Push-i-can" or "Pur-
> chi-can," another war chief of the Snakes, bears upon his forehead the scar of a
> blow of the tomahawk given by Washikee in one of these altercations. Washikee,
> who is also known by the term of "the white man's friend," was many years ago
> in the employment of the American and Hudson's Bay Fur Companies. He was
> the constant companion of the white trappers, and his superior knowledge and
> accomplishments may be attributed to this fact.

Other names than that of Washakie are noted among the lists of chiefs in Wyoming and Utah during the early 1860's. Among the Indians reported killed at Bear River in 1863 were Bear Hunter, Sagwich, and Leight (War of the Rebellion, 1902, p. 187). In the same source, the chiefs Pocatello and San Pitch were said to be still at large. These chiefs were usually in Utah and were independent of Washakie's band, although the relations between Wyoming and Bear River would suggest considerable interchange, even inseparability, of population. The virtual impossibility of dividing bands and populations during this period is indicated by Doty's list of the participants in the Fort Bridger Treaty of 1863. Doty claimed that between three and four thousand Indians were represented by the signatories and over one thousand people were present at the treaty (1865, p. 319):

> They are known as Waushakee's band (who is the principal chief of the nation),
> Wonapitz's band, Shauwuno's band, Tibagan's band, Peoastogah's band, Totimee's
> band, Ashingodimah's band (he was killed at the battle on Bear River) Sagowitz's
> band (wounded at the same battle) Oretzimawik's band, Bazil's band, Sanpitz's band.
> The bands of this chief and of Sagowitz were nearly exterminated in the same battle.

In a later compendium of chiefs Powell and Ingalls listed Sanpits as a Cache Valley chief over a group of 124, Sai-guits as the leader of 158 Shoshone also in Cache Valley, Tav-i-wun-shean as headman at Bear Lake with 17 people, and Po-ka-tel-lo as chief over 101 Indians at Goose Creek (Powell and Ingalls, 1874, p. 419).

Washakie evidently owed his position to a combination of his status as a war-leader, as a recognized intermediary with the whites, and as an unusually strong personality. However, as we shall see later, there were other chiefs among the Wyoming Shoshone, and Washakie's position, although always strong, was never completely unchallenged. Much of his strength derived from recognition by the whites, and the government officials made every effort to bolster Washakie's prestige actively. Lander, for example, urged: "Any steps which could be taken to augment the power of Washakee, who is perfectly safe in his attachment to the Americans and northern mountaineers, would also prove beneficial" (Lander, 1860, p. 123). Also, Agent Mann reported in 1868 the deviation of many Shoshone from Washakie's leadership in the following terms (1869, p. 618):

> This diminution of his strength is not satisfactory to Washakie; hence I have instructed all who have the means and are not too aged belonging to these bands to follow Washakie, impressing them with the fact that he alone is recognized as their head, and assuring them that if they expect to share the reward they must participate in all dangers incident to the tribe. [Mann refers to residence on the often attacked Wind River Reservation.]

This situation grew worse shortly after the treaty. Mann reported in 1869 (1870, p. 716): "A strong party is now separated from Washakie, and under the leadership of a half-breed, who has always sustained a good character, but who is, nevertheless, crafty and somewhat ambitious." Mann's successor. Captain J. H. Patterson, said in the same year. (Patterson, 1870, p. 717):

> Washakie, the head chief, is rapidly losing his influence in the tribe, though he has yet the larger band under his immediate command; all or nearly all of the young men are with the other chiefs. This division looks badly.

He goes on to identify some of these chiefs (ibid.):

> Shortly after my arrival [June 24, 1869] Nar-kok's band of Shoshones came in to receive their goods. Washakie's, Tab-on-she-ya's, and Bazil's bands were near at hand.

The size of these bands is indicated in the following year, when Agent Fleming commented that Washakie's people "were joined by Tab-en-shen and Bazil, with about 64 lodges" (G. W. Fleming, 1871, p. 644). However, Washakie maintained his position of spokesman for the Eastern Shoshone. Governor J. A. Campbell claimed in 1870 (1871, p. 639):

> Wash-a-kie ... has great influence with his tribe, which I have endeavored to retain for him by always recognizing him as their chief, and referring all others of his tribe to him as the only one through whom I can hold any communication with them.

Wind River Shoshone informants showed more confusion over chieftainship and patterns of leadership, in general, than on any other subject. All knew of Washakie and recognized his chieftaincy, but of those chiefs mentioned in sources confirmation was received only of Nar-kok, and this from but one informant. Shimkin mentions four main bands, each with its own chief (1947*a*, p. 247):

> The band led by Ta'wunasia would go down the Sweetwater to the upper North Platte [for the buffalo hunt]. That led by Di'kandimp went straight east to the Powder River Valley; that led by No'oki skirted the base of the Big Horn Mountains, passing through Crow territory, then swung south again to the Powder River Valley. Washakie ascended Big Wind River, and then crossed the divide to winter near the headquarters of the Greybull.

Except for Washakie, No'oki was the only one of the above chiefs given also by our informants. Parenthetically, it should be emphasized that most of our informants stated that all the Eastern Shoshone hunted buffalo together for self-protection. The preceding historical account also suggests that Shimkin's data do not represent a stable traditional pattern, since the Plains were almost untenable until after the treaty, except for short hunts in strength.

The following is a list of Wind River chiefs in the early reservation period, as given by informants. It should be remembered that a man might have more than one name, and phonetic transcriptions usually vary according to the recorder (and the informant).

Wantsea
Wanhi (Wantni)
Ohata (Ohotwe)
Dupeshipöoi (Dupíshibowoi)
Dabunesiu
Bohowansiye (Bohowosa)
Witungak
Dönotsi
Noki (No'oki of Shimkin)
Wohowat
Yohodökatsi
Noiohugo
Tagi
Tishawa
Wahawiichi
Sunup
Nakok (Narkok)

Washakie was mentioned by most informants as the head chief of the Eastern Shoshone. One old woman, however, said that he was more of a chief in the eyes of the whites than among the Shoshone; another commented that there were many chiefs, but that only Washakie was known by the whites. Washakie's most important function was to represent the Shoshone before the whites; this is understandable since the whites would deal with nobody else.

It was also commonly agreed that Washakie led the collective buffalo hunt, although the oldest man on the reservation claimed that there were many chiefs and that there was no special leader for the buffalo hunt. Informants said, furthermore, that the head chief acted as such only during those times of the year when all the people were together. Some stated that he directed them to the winter encampment and told them where to go in springtime and summer. Washakie was said to have acted at these times in council with the lesser chiefs and decisions were made known to the camp through an announcer. One informant said that Noki (No'oki) acted as announcer. The statement that Washakie assigned summer hunting areas to bands is undoubtedly erroneous, for it conflicts with the testimony of most informants that each group went where it chose.

There was also disagreement on the extent of Washakie's influence. According to some informants, the term "Buffalo Eaters," as applied to Washakie's Wind River band, did not denote the people in the Green River country. Wanhi was said to be the chief of the people in the Fort Bridger area and not Washakie, who was chief only in Wind River. This division probably refers to the split between those who chose to settle on the reservation and those who did not.

Despite considerable confusion about the role of the subchiefs, or lesser chiefs, they appear to have been men of prestige who had their own small following, although they recognized the personal influence of Washakie during large gatherings and general band endeavors. When not on the buffalo hunt or in winter camp these smaller groups of families, led by one or two of the minor leaders, functioned autonomously. Their itineraries and activities have already been described.

The small band was undoubtedly a much more basic unit in Eastern Shoshone society than the "tribe" as a whole. Intermarriage linked the small camp groups, although one could marry into his own unit if incest rules, as determined by kinship bonds, were not violated. There was no obligatory rule of residence, but the couple more frequently resided after marriage with the bride's family. This was not necessarily a permanent arrangement, and visits were made to the families of either mate for extended periods. This, combined with individual freedom of choice of band membership, caused affiliations to be shifting and fluid. Ultimately these Shoshone were bilocal and neolocal. As has been said, the bands were not territory-owning units, and their chief functions were to provide economic coöperation and defense against enemies.

Leadership was an attained status and was not transmitted by descent. Raynolds, however, refers to Cut-Nose as being the "hereditary chief of the Snakes," according to information received from Jim Bridger (Raynolds, 1868, p. 95), and the reservation chieftaincy passed patrilineally in Washakie's family until the Reorganization Act established the tribal council. However, all informants agreed that one became a chief owing to merit-primarily through renown as a warrior. That the chieftaincy was neither inherited nor permanent is indicated by the proliferation of chiefs' names in historical sources. Except for such figures as Washakie and Pocatello, a chief is rarely mentioned twice, and it can be hypothesized that many were the leaders of ephemeral predatory bands that arose for specific purposes of defense or agression against the whites and dissolved shortly after the period of emergency passed. Finally, any man who had achieved renown and prestige or was the leader of a camp group, was known as a "chief," for the lack of institutionalization and formalization of the office made its tenure most nebulous.

It was not even necessary that a Shoshone chief be a Shoshone. During 1858, we hear of a Delaware Indian named Ben Simons, undoubtedly a former fur trapper, who was at the head of some 150-400 Shoshone on the upper Bear River (Gove, 1928, pp. 133, 146, 277). And Washakie, himself, was born into the Flathead tribe. Washakie's Flathead father was killed by the Blackfoot, and his mother sought refuge with the Lemhi River Shoshone of Idaho. He eventually gained renown in the Green and Bear River country as a warrior and attained his final position as a successful mediator with the whites.

Finally, Washakie's career gives additional evidence that there were no hard and fast lines between the so-called "Eastern Shoshone" and other Shoshone groups. Washakie's wanderings, according to Wilson, took him into Utah, Idaho, and Montana (E. N. Wilson, 1926, pp. 68-73). This was consistent with the general Shoshone pattern of visiting between areas for short or extended periods. The unique character of Washakie's leadership can best be explained in terms of contact with the whites and the Shoshones' need to expand into the buffalo grounds east of the Rocky Mountains. First, Washakie united and represented all those Shoshone who did not choose to join their fellows in northern Utah and southern Idaho in hostilities against the whites. Second, Washakie was an able and vigorous war leader under whom the embattled Shoshone could rally. Although at no time a separate, territorially distinct and exclusive group, the Eastern Shoshone evidently became somewhat differentiated from their people to the west by the latter's long distance from the shrinking buffalo grounds and by their distaste for the warlike activities of their Utah and Idaho fellows. The Eastern Shoshone, however, did not attempt to maintain the area over which they roamed to the exclusion of other Shoshone and of the Bannock. Their neighbors and colinguists to the west, if they were properly mounted, could and did join with them in buffalo hunting.

III. THE SHOSHONE AND BANNOCK OF IDAHO

The Shoshone of western Wyoming were a mobile population whose primary subsistence was provided by buffalo herds. The Shoshone of Idaho showed no such unity of ecological adaptation, for the region was inhabited by mounted buffalo hunters and by less prosperous Shoshone who fished and gathered wild vegetables for a livelihood. While the buffalo hunters tended to be located in the southeastern part of Idaho and the fishing and gathering peoples in the southwestern, the mounted hunters traveled throughout the southern part of the state and, at certain times of the year, mingled with the poorer, footgoing Indians.

Because of this diversity we have divided Idaho into six subregions and present the historical and ethnographic data pertinent to each area under a separate heading. Indians mentioned in the historical sources are not always easily identifiable as Shoshone, Bannock, or Northern Paiute, and a great deal of confusion between the last two is inherent in their linguistic bond. We shall use the name Bannock in its most common sense to designate the mounted, buffalo-hunting Mono-Bannock speakers of Idaho; Northern Paiute refers specifically to the Mono-Bannock population to the west of the Shoshone. In many instances we cannot be certain that the Indians encountered by one or another traveler were permanent residents of the area. Permanency, in any event, is a rather doubtful attribute of this highly nomadic people; the term cannot be used except as a designation for the people who customarily spend the winter in a certain area, and even with this limitation it must be used with caution.

LINGUISTICS

All of the groups discussed in this chapter except the Bannock speak the Shoshone-Comanche, or Shoshone, language. While there were only minor differences of dialect between Shoshone speakers, the Bannock language was almost identical with Northern Paiute. Informants found an especially close affinity between Bannock and the language of the Oregon Paiute, who were frequently referred to as "Bannock" also and were sometimes distinguished from the Fort Hall Bannock only by the statement that "they live in Burns" (a town in Oregon). While some informants referred to the Oregon speakers of Mono-Bannock as "Paiute," this term was generally reserved for the population of west-central Nevada, and "Pyramid Lake" was the locale in which the Idaho Shoshone generally placed the "Paiute." The inhabitants of Duck Valley Indian Reservation were not so vague; they readily distinguished between Shoshone and "Paiute" on linguistic and other grounds. This is understandable because the Shoshone had lived a long time on the same reservation as the Oregon speakers of Mono-Bannock, who were officially designated as Paiute. While no vocabularies were collected on the Fort Hall Reservation among either the Shoshone or Bannock populations, data from informants on the similarity of Paiute and Bannock more than confirm Steward's statement (1938, p. 198):

> The linguistic similarity of the Bannock and Northern Paiute (see vocabularies, pp. 274-275) leaves no doubt that they once formed a single group, though within historic times they have been separated by 200 miles.

The vocabularies to which Steward refers were taken from Northern Paiute at Mill City, a town southwest of Winnemucca, Nevada, and at George's Creek, in Owens Valley, California. It is probable that correspondences would have been even closer if vocabularies had been taken among the Northern Paiute of Oregon, for Fort Hall Bannock informants specifically stated that their language was more akin to that of the Oregon Paiute; the Pyramid Lake people were said to "talk fast" or "talk funny." The frequent designation of the Oregon Paiute as "Bannock" by both Bannock and Shoshone at Fort Hall Reservation bespeaks the linguistic similarity or virtual identity of the languages of the respective groups.

As for Shoshone and Bannock, the two languages were not sufficiently similar to be mutually intelligible, although there are a great many cognate words. However, they were not so far removed from one another as to make bilingualism difficult. There was considerable bilingualism among the population of the Fort Hall plains.

GENERAL DISTRIBUTION OF POPULATION

The following division of the Shoshone-Bannock population of Idaho into six main groups is admittedly arbitrary, although to a certain extent the sectors conform to actual sociopolitical groups or to populations designated by certain characteristics recognized by the Indians themselves. Proceeding from west to east, these are: (1) the population of the Boise and Weiser River valleys; (2) the Shoshone Indians of the middle course of the Snake River between Glenn's Ferry and Shoshone Falls and in the interior on both sides of the river; (3) the Shoshone of the Sawtooth Mountains, west of the Lemhi River, Idaho; (4) the population of Bannock Creek, Idaho, and south therefrom to Bear River; (5) the Shoshone and Bannock of the Fort Hall plains on the upper Snake River; and (6) the Shoshone Indians of the Lemhi River.

It will be seen that the Shoshone population of Idaho was by no means a unitary one, either socially or culturally. The people of these six areas were not politically interrelated, nor were the populations of each area integrated social or political units, although the Fort Hall and Lemhi River people were more highly organized than those of other areas. On the contrary, the Indians subsumed under each of the six divisions primarily consist of people who lived under similar ecological conditions and dwelt in geographical contiguity. Some shared roughly the same nomadic pattern and united upon occasion for diverse reasons. The populations represented by our sixfold division interacted more frequently for economic, social, and religious purposes with people within the area than they did with those from other areas.

Although strong patterns of leadership and a tightly nucleated society were alien to the Shoshone in general, the Shoshone gave verbal recognition to the more frequent interaction that existed between neighboring families or camp groups, especially when such neighborhoods were geographically discontinuous with other neighborhoods. Also, differences in food resources and habits of peoples of certain demarcated ecological provinces apparently impressed other Shoshone as significant criteria by which the people of these neighborhoods could be named. This is the only logical explanation for the common pattern among Northern Paiute and Shoshone of the Great Basin of food names applied to the people of certain neighborhoods. Thus we have "Wada Seed Eaters," "Salmon Eaters," etc. In fact, it was quite common for the populations so designated to call themselves by these names, although this was not always so. In any event, it would be erroneous to say that such appellations implied membership in any social group, whether defined by united political leadership or by kinship. That individual families subsumed under some name, usually derived from food habits, tended to act more frequently together than with more distant neighbors cannot be denied, nor can we ignore the fact that common environment tended to induce a common subsistence pattern. That such groups were organized, territory-holding units cannot be simply assumed without supporting evidence, and this evidence is lacking. This view is shared by Steward, who summarizes the political significance of the food names in the following passage (Steward, 1939, p. 262):

> The emphasis, I think, is clearly upon the territory rather than upon any unified group of people occupying it. The extent of the people so designated depended upon the extent of the geographical feature or food in question. A name might apply to a single village, a valley, or a number of valleys. Some Snake River Shoshone vaguely called all Nevada Shoshone Pine Nut Eaters, the pinyon nut not occurring in Idaho. Furthermore, several names might be used for the same people. This system of nomenclature served in a crude way to identify people by their habitat. Upon moving to new localities, they acquired new names.

In general, the remarks above apply to our Boise-Weiser, Bannock Creek, middle Snake River, and Sawtooth Mountains populations and to the Shoshone of Nevada. The Indians of the Fort Hall plains and the Lemhi River were somewhat different. Both had horses at a relatively early period, were involved in frequent wars, and pursued the buffalo. These factors tended to promote a somewhat different sociopolitical organization than we find farther west. Band organization, however fluid and shifting, did exist in the Fort Hall and Lemhi areas.

Finally, it should be remembered that the Indians of our six regions frequently wandered far from the areas designated. The areas, then, were centers of gravity in a migratory life. They were areas where subsistence was commonly obtained by the populations in question and, more important, where winter, the most sedentary season of the year, was passed.

THE BOISE AND WEISER RIVERS

The region of the Boise, Payette, and Weiser rivers and the near-by shores of the Snake River are of considerable importance because of the contiguity of Shoshone and Northern Paiute populations in this area. We will present the historical data pertinent to an understanding of the mode and extent of Shoshone ecology there and will then give the material gathered through recent ethnographic investigation.

Our earliest information on this region comes from the Stuart diary of the Astoria party. Stuart wrote of the Boise River (1935, p. 83):

> ... the most renowned Fishing place in this Country. It is consequently the resort
> of the majority of the Snakes, where immense numbers of Salmon are taken.

The Hunt party arrived at the Boise River on November 21, 1811, and met well-clad and mounted Indians there (ibid., p. 295). One week later, the party came to Mann's Creek, a tributary of the Weiser River, and there found "some huts of Chochonis" (p. 296):

> They had just killed two young horses to eat. It is their only food except for the
> seed of a plant which resembles hemp and which they pound very fine.

In the mountains between Mann's Creek and the Snake River some dozen huts of "Chochonies" were encountered (p. 299); the journals use Snake and "Chochoni" or "Shoshonie" interchangeably.

The 1818-19 journals of Alexander Ross gave considerable attention to hostilities between the "Snakes" and the Sahaptin ("Shaw-ha-ap-tens")-speaking peoples (Ross, 1924, pp. 171, 210, 214). Part of this action took place in southwestern Idaho. Ross attempted to arrange peace between the hostile populations and wrote of a council held there under the chiefs "Pee-eye-em" and "Ama-qui-em" and participated in by the "Shirry-dikas," "War-are-ree-kas," and "Ban-at-tees" (p. 243). The two chiefs, said by Ross to be brothers, were previously mentioned as the "principal chiefs" of "the great Snake nation" (p. 238). They belonged to the people called "Shirry-dika," a buffalo-hunting population, for Ross spoke of the acquiescence of "Ama-ketsa," a chief of the "War-are-ree-kas" (fish-eaters, according to Ross), in the maintenance of peace and the cowing of the "Ban-at-tees" by the two leaders (p. 246). Ross represents the Shoshone as having a very large population; those at the peace conference were said to have stretched their camps along both sides of a stream for a distance of seven miles. The "Shirry-dikas" are depicted as the most powerful, and the "War-are-ree-kas," though numerous, are said to lack power and unity. The "Ban-at-tees, or Mountain Snakes" are described as a fragmented population, living in the mountain fastnesses and preying upon the trappers. This seems to characterize the Northern Paiute of Oregon more accurately than the mounted buffalo-hunting Bannock of southeastern Idaho.

The journal of John Work in June, 1832, mentioned (Work, 1923, pp. 165-167) "Snake" Indians on the Payette River, immediately below the mouth of Big Willow Creek; on Little Willow Creek; on the Weiser River; and on the east bank of the Snake River, between the mouths of the Payette and the Weiser. Work used the term Snake in a broad sense and we cannot identify this population as Shoshone with certainty. The Indians had horses, and may thus have been a buffalo-hunting group that had traveled west for salmon. Nathaniel Wyeth entered one of the western Idaho valleys in October of the same year and observed "extensive camps of Indians about one month old. Here they find salmon in a creek running through it and dig the Kamas root but not an Indian was here at this time" (Wyeth, 1899, p. 172). Wyeth was on the Boise River in August, 1834, and encountered "a small village of Snakes." His party proceeded on to the Snake River where they found "a few lodges of very impudent Pawnacks" (p. 229). "Bannock" Indians were also encountered on the Boise River in 1833 by Bonneville's party (Irving, 1837, 2:38) and in the following year his journals noted that "formidable bands of the Banneck Indians were lying on the Boisée and Payette Rivers" (p. 194). The Bannock, or the Indians so termed by our sources, evidently lived near the confluence of these streams with the Snake River, for John Townsend, a young naturalist who joined Wyeth's party, reported several groups of about twenty Indians fishing in the Boise River each of which identified itself as Shoshone (Townsend, 1905, pp. 206-207). Farther down the Boise River the party "came to a village consisting of thirty willow lodges of the Pawnees (Bannocks)" (p. 210). The Shoshone and the Mono-Bannock speakers did not maintain complete separateness, however, for Townsend wrote (1905, p. 266) that the party met some ten lodges of "Snakes and Bannecks" on the west side of the Snake River, near Burnt River.

The identity of the above-mentioned Bannock is somewhat doubtful. Farnham met a number of Shoshone Indians engaged in fishing the Boise River in September, 1839 (Farnham, 1843, pp. 75-76). Some thirty traveling miles downstream from Boise, however, he noted in apparent contradiction of Townsend, that there were no more "Shoshonie," for "they dare not pass the boundary line between themselves and the Bonacks." The Bannock are described as a "fierce, warlike, and athletic tribe inhabiting that part of Saptin or Snake River which lies between the mouth of Boisais or Reed's River and the Blue Mountains." The question arises whether the Bannock mentioned in the sources were the buffalo-hunting Mono-Bannock speakers who regularly inhabited the upper Snake River or whether they followed the fishing and seed-collecting pattern of the Mono-Bannock speakers of Oregon. Townsend's report of their use of willow lodges suggests that they were Mono-Bannock, but Farnham observed that the Bannock found on the Snake River made war on the Crow and Blackfoot (p. 76). This would definitely suggest life during part of the year in southeastern Idaho and, also, the pursuit of the buffalo. Later historical data and the testimony of contemporary informants suggest that both the Oregon and eastern Idaho populations of Mono-Bannock speakers fished on the Snake River and in the lower reaches of the Boise and Weiser rivers. There was no clear boundary between the Shoshone and the Oregon people termed Northern Paiute, and the mounted buffalo-hunting Bannock also visited western Idaho to fish for salmon. It is thus doubtful whether the ambiguities of the historical sources will ever be resolved.

The subsequent historical references to the native population of this region cover the outbreak of hostilities against the white emigrants on the Oregon Trail and the subsequent attempts to establish peace with the Indians and place them on reservations. In 1862 Special Indian Agent Kirkpatrick surveyed the southwestern Idaho Indians and reported: "The Winnas band of Snakes inhabit the country north of Snake river, and are found principally on the Bayette, Boise and Sickley Rivers" (Kirkpatrick, 1863, p. 412). He reported them as warlike and numbering some 700 to 800 people. Kirkpatrick's "Winnas band" probably corresponds to the designation of the "Wihinasht" in the Handbook of American Indians; these are said to be "a division of Shoshoni, formerly in western Idaho, north of Snake River and in the vicinity of Boise City" (Hodge, 1910, 2:951). During our field work, we found that the term "Wihinait" was often applied generically to the Shoshone population of Fort Hall Reservation.

In later years, other bands are reported in southwestern Idaho. Governor Caleb Lyon made a treaty with "San-to-me-co and the headmen of the Boise Shoshonees" on October 10, 1864 (Lyon, 1866, p. 418) and in the following year placed some 115 "Boise Shoshone" at Fort Boise (Lyon, 1867, p. 187). Special Indian Agent Hough mentioned Boise, Bruneau, and Kammas bands of Shoshone in 1866 and commented: "The Bruneau and Boise are so intermarried that they are in fact all one people and are closely connected by blood, visiting each other as frequently as they dare pass over the country" (Hough, 1867, p. 189). Governor Ballard, in the same year, reported that the "Boise Shoshones" numbered 200; insecurity due to Indian-white hostilities kept them from camas-root digging during the summer (Ballard, 1867, p. 190). In 1867 many Shoshone of the Boise and Bruneau rivers and a group of Bannock were placed temporarily on the Boise River, some thirty miles upstream from Boise (Powell, 1868, p. 252). The Bannock were said to have been under the leadership of a chief named "Bannock John"; the report, dated July 31, 1867, also mentioned that these Bannock engaged in salmon fishing in the

Boise River and camas collection on Camas Prairie during the summer, but intended to go east for the buffalo hunt in the fall. That the above Bannock were mounted buffalo hunters rather than Oregon Paiute seems manifest from this statement. This was not the only Bannock band, however, for on July 15, 1867, Agent Mann of Fort Bridger, Wyoming, reported a conversation with "Tahjee, the chief of the Bannacks" in which he learned that "there does exist a very large band of Bannacks, numbering more than 100 lodges" (Mann, 1868, p. 189). Mann stated that 50 lodges of these Indians were present that year. This and other references to the diverse, but simultaneous, locations of the Bannock suggest that they were not a unitary political entity.

References to the Bannock and to the Shoshone on the Boise and Bruneau rivers continue during the next two years. Powell gave their numbers in 1868 as 100, 283, and 300, respectively, and stated (C. F. Powell, 1869, p. 662):

> ... [the Bannock] remained under my charge for several months, when they were permitted to go on their regular buffalo hunt, their country ranging through eastern Idaho and Montana. When through their hunt they return to the Boise and Bruneau camp; they and the Boise and Bruneau are on the best of terms, all being more or less intermarried.

Ballard reported that on August 26, 1867, a treaty was signed by Tygee, Peter, To-so-copy-natey, Pah Vissigin, McKay, and Jim, in which the Bannock agreed to settle on Fort Hall (Ballard, 1869, p. 658); the Bannock and also the Bruneau and Boise Shoshone were removed from the Boise Valley on December 2, 1868, and brought to Fort Hall (C. F. Powell, 1870, p. 728). They were joined there by 500 Bannock under Tygee, who had just returned from a joint buffalo hunt with the Eastern Shoshone in Wind River Valley (p. 729). Indian Agent Danilson of Fort Hall wrote that in 1869 there were 600 Bannock, 200 Boise Shoshone, 100 Bruneau Shoshone, and 200 Western Shoshone on the reservation (Danilson, 1870, p. 729). The beginning of the reservation period marks the effective end of the independent occupancy of the Idaho area by the Shoshone and Bannock. The rest of this section deals with ethnographic data. In regard to extent of Shoshone settlement, Omer Stewart has reported that eastern Oregon, about the mouths of the Malheur and Owyhee rivers, and southwest Idaho as far east as a line well past Boise, were the territory of a Northern Paiute band called the Koa'agaitoka (Stewart, 1939, p. 133). Blythe places a Northern Paiute band called "Yapa Eaters" in the Boise River Valley (Blythe, 1938, p. 396) and mentions data given by one informant to the effect that a mixed band of Paiute and Shoshone called "People Eaters" lived to the north of the Yapa Eaters (p. 404). Neither historical research nor ethnographic investigation among the Shoshone confirms the existence of such bands in the area described. On the contrary, Steward writes (1938, p. 172):

> Shoshone seem to have extended westward about to the Snake River which forms the boundary between Idaho and Oregon. They also occupied the Boise River Valley and probably to some extent the valleys of the Payette and Weiser Rivers. They probably never penetrated Oregon beyond the Blue Mountains.

But the area nearer the Snake River was not occupied exclusively by Shoshone, for Steward continues (ibid.):

> This population was neither well defined politically nor territorially. It was scattered in small independent villages of varying prosperity and tribal composition. Along the lower Snake, Boise, and Payette Rivers Shoshone were intermixed with Northern Paiute who extended westward through the greater portion of southern and eastern Oregon. Slightly to the north they were probably mixed somewhat with their Nez Percé neighbors.

Our own field work, as presented below, tends to confirm Steward's data on most points and is in accord with historical information.

Although there were salmon-yielding streams in Oregon, the Boise and Weiser rivers were richer in these fish, and salmon could be caught on the Boise River upstream to its headwaters. During the spring and fall salmon runs, many Northern Paiute evidently crossed the Snake River and fished in the Boise and Weiser. Relations seem to have been friendly, and there was considerable intermarriage. Many Paiute evidently wintered in this area and could therefore be said to be as regular residents as the Shoshone. They maintained separate winter villages and tended to remain along the downstream stretches of the Boise and Weiser rivers. Informants disagreed on the extent of this interpenetration. Some characterized the population, especially of the Weiser Valley, as "mixed," while others said that only a very few Northern Paiute remained through the winter. More reliable and older informants characterized the population as mostly Shoshone. One old woman, a present resident of Duck Valley Reservation, identified herself as a Northern Paiute from the Weiser country. Her conversation, however, immediately revealed that she was actually speaking in the Shoshone language and that this was her first language. This attempted deception is partially explained by the somewhat greater prestige enjoyed by the Northern Paiute on that reservation.

As has been mentioned, the composition of the population of this region is further confused by the fact that some camp groups of Bannock passed by the more commonly used fishing sites below Shoshone Falls and fished on the Boise and Weiser rivers. An added inducement to the Bannock was the possibility of trade with the Nez Percé Indians in the upper valley of the Weiser River. The Bannock did not stay long in the area, however, and never wintered there.

The Boise-Weiser country is relatively rich. The streams gave a good yield of fish, roots abounded in the valleys, and game was found in the near-by mountains. The floors of the valleys are well below 3,000 feet, and winters are comparatively mild. Although the Shoshone residents of the area wandered far on occasion, a full subsistence could be obtained within the immediate area. Stretches of mountainous and barren lands tended to mark off this population from other Shoshone to the east. The testimony of informants is somewhat contradictory to Steward's statement (1938, p. 172) that the Boise-Weiser Shoshone "imperceptibly merged with the Agaidüka of the Snake River and the Tukadüka of the mountains to the north." It is true that there were no concepts of territorial boundaries and that the above-mentioned populations interacted, interchanged, and interpenetrated, but the locus of movement of each of the above three populations, especially their wintering places, did differ.

While Steward reports that the rubric "Yahandüka," or "Groundhog Eaters," was applied to the residents of the Boise-Weiser areas, we were unable to obtain this name. Yahandika was variously reported by Fort Hall informants as referring to a district in Nevada; by others as applied to certain Oregon Northern Paiute. Another informant said that it was an alternate term for the Shoshone of the middle Snake River, who are more generally called "Summer Salmon Eaters." The latter, stated this informant, had very close relations with the Boise population. All of the informants were probably right in a sense; only the uncertainty of these appellations is indicated.

Steward obtained "Su:woki" as the name of the Boise-Weiser country. My informants applied this name to the people of the region also, who were called "Söhuwawki," or "Row of Willows." The place name had evidently been transferred to the people or, more accurately, the place name was applied to whatever people used the locale. The name was especially used to denote the people and country of the Weiser River, although one informant thought the name covered the Boise people also. Another name given to the Weiser Shoshone was "Woviagaidika," or "Driftwood Salmon Eaters." This name is derived from the salmon's habit of lying under the driftwood in small streams. Only one informant reported a name for the dwellers of the Boise Valley, "Pa avi."

Informants sometimes spoke of the Boise-Weiser Shoshone as being "just one bunch." Certainly the populations of this section of Idaho merged, shifted, and interacted to such an extent that it would be difficult to distinguish them, although "one bunch," two chiefs, Captain Jim and Eagle Eye, were reported for the area. The former was said to be chief of those who usually wintered in the vicinity of Boise; the latter was chief of the winter residents of the Weiser valley. No clear delineation of the functions of these chiefs could be obtained.

The actual nature of Boise-Weiser Shoshone society can be understood better from their subsistence patterns. Winter was spent in small camps scattered along the valleys of the streams. There was little danger from hostile intruders, and camp grounds were not the larger population nuclei that we find in the Fort Hall area. Favorite winter camp sites were at the present site of the city of Boise, near present-day Emmett on the Payette River, and on the lower Weiser River, near the mouth of Crane Creek. Some families were said to have wintered on both sides of the near-by Snake River. While it was common for the same families to form winter camp groups, there was considerable shifting and changing each year, dictated by personal preference. Also, it was not necessary for the camps to spend every winter in the same place, and changes occurred constantly.

Winter was spent by their caches of roots and salmon; the dried and jerked game meat was said to have been kept in the lodge. The common type of winter dwelling was a sort of tipi made of rye grass. Stored food supplied the main subsistence during the winter, but sagehens, blue grouse, and snowshoe rabbits were also taken. Antelope were chased on horses (probably by the surround method), and deer frequently came down from the mountains and were killed while floundering in deep snow.

Springtime brought no extensive migrations. Some roots were available in the area, but the chief source of springtime subsistence was the salmon run, which began in approximately March or April. A second run followed immediately upon the first and continued until the end of spring. Fish traps were made on the Payette River, in the vicinity of Long Valley, and on the lower Weiser River. Salmon were also taken in the Boise River. According to informants, the people of this area did not resort to the great salmon fisheries in the vicinity of Glenn's Ferry and upstream to Shoshone Falls. The abundance of fish in local waters made this unnecessary. Although the population divided and went to various fishing sites, the salmon runs were periods during which stable residence in small villages was possible.

At the end of spring and in early summer, many of the Indians of the Boise-Weiser country traveled to Camas Prairie, where roots of various kinds were dug. These people stayed there through part of the summer, and during this time roots were collected and dried. This was also a time of dances and festivities, for a large part of the Shoshone and Bannock population of Idaho, plus a sprinkling of the Nez Percé and Flathead, resorted at the same time to these root grounds. These were probably the largest gatherings of people among all the Shoshone. There was no large, single encampment, but families and camp groups were in such close contiguity that social interaction was intense.

At the conclusion of the root-collecting season at Camas Prairie, the inhabitants of the Boise and Weiser region wandered back to their customary area and set out upon their late summer and fall activities. Fish were taken during the fall run and dried for winter provisions, but the chief activity was hunting. Both hunting and fishing could be pursued at the same time in the upper waters of the Boise and Payette rivers, although salmon did not ascend far up the Weiser. Hunting was done by small camp groups of 3 to 4 lodges, and the population scattered throughout the mountain country surrounding the river valleys. The principal game taken was deer, elk, bear, and some bighorn sheep. None required the collective efforts of a large number of men, and all were found throughout the mountain area. The small camp group was, therefore, the most effective social unit for the fall hunt, as it was for the summer wanderings of the Wyoming Shoshone.

The hunters ranged up the Boise and Payette valleys into the Sawtooth Mountains as far as the beginnings of the Salmon River watershed. Though the Salmon River country was entered, the hunting parties did not penetrate very far. A favored hunting territory was in the Stanley Basin, at the headwaters of the Salmon River and in the vicinity of the present-day village of Stanley. The kill of game was dried in the mountains and packed down to the winter quarters in the valleys of the Boise, Payette, and Weiser rivers.

In general, it is difficult to define the social organization of the Boise-Weiser Shoshone. While Shoshone social organization is characteristically amorphous, some groups developed a closer integration owing to such factors as warfare and collective economic activities, which demanded leadership. But warfare was rare in this region, and hunting and root-and berry-collecting were essentially carried on by families. The building and operation of fish traps and the distribution of the catch undoubtedly called forth some leadership functions, but not on the band level. Also, the presence of other groups which fished the same streams during the appropriate seasons seems to argue against the consolidation of either the Boise or Weiser people into territorially delimited bands. It was impossible to elicit exact information from informants on the functions of leaders, and it can only be inferred that they probably served as intermediaries with the whites or were simply local men enjoying some prestige as dance directors or leaders of winter villages.

The Shoshone of this area were poorer in horses than the buffalo hunters, but they did possess some. The valleys of the Boise, Payette, and Weiser evidently afforded adequate grazing for small herds, and the natives enjoyed a greater mobility than did their neighbors to the northeast and southeast. The resulting ease of communication would perhaps be conducive to band organization, but neither living informants nor historical sources offer any confirmation of this. That such sociopolitical groups did exist is suggested by mention of chiefs, but the groups did not have clearly defined territories which excluded other peoples, and they could only have been most loosely organized.

THE MIDDLE SNAKE RIVER

This area includes all of Idaho south of the Sawtooth Mountains between American Falls and the Bruneau River. It has been seen that the area of the Boise, Payette, and Weiser rivers was entered regularly by populations that did not customarily winter there; this is true also of the area of the middle Snake, and to a much greater degree. First, the salmon run did not extend above Shoshone Falls, and the population living upstream from that point resorted regularly to favored fishing places below the Falls. Second, the prairies about the locale of present-day Fairfield, Idaho, were the richest camas-root grounds in this section of the Basin-Plateau area and large numbers of Indians convened every summer to gather the roots. Historical sources testify to the numbers of Indians found in the area during certain times of the year, but it is usually impossible to determine the geographical locus of these people during the remainder of the year.

Travelers observed small, impoverished groups of Indians and also larger camps of mounted people. Near Glenn's Ferry, Idaho, Stuart on August 23, 1812, noted (1935, p. 108):

> ...a few Shoshonie (or Snake) Camps were passed today, who have to struggle hard
> for a livelihood, even though it is the prime of the fishing season in the Country.

Stuart encountered some 100 lodges of Shoshone fishing at Salmon Falls (p. 109). In 1826 Peter Skene Ogden met a camp of 200 "Snakes" bearing 60 firearms and a quantity of ammunition at Raft River, above the limit of the salmon run (Ogden, 1909, p. 357). In October of the following year he visited Camas Prairie, the camas grounds in the vicinity of Fairfield, and noted a pattern of movement that is still reported by informants (p. 263):

> It is from near this point the Snakes form into a body prior to their starting point
> for buffalo; they collect camasse for the journey across the mountains. Their camp
> is 300 tents. In Spring they scattered from this place for the salmon and horse
> thieving expeditions.

Buffalo were formerly found on the plains of the upper Snake River, but American Falls was apparently their approximate western limit. Wyeth was at American Falls in August, 1832, and wrote (1899, p. 163):

> We found here plenty of Buffaloe sign and the Pawnacks come here to winter often
> on account of the Buffaloe we now find no buffaloe.

The Wyeth party then turned up the Raft River where they "met a village of the Snakes of about 150 persons having about 75 horses" and farther upstream found "the banks lined with Diggers Camps and Trails but they are shy and can seldom be spoken." On Rock Creek, the party met some 120 Indians who evidently had fresh salmon, and farther on their journey on this stream they found "Diggers," "Sohonees," and "Pawnacks" (ibid., pp. 166-168). A chief and some sub-chiefs were mentioned at one of these camps. Small and scattered camps of Indians were mentioned throughout Wyeth's journeys on the southern tributaries of the Snake River.

Fewer Indians were encountered in the salmon-yielding sections of the Snake River during the winter. Bonneville's party met only footgoing Indians near Salmon Falls in the winter of 1834; the Indians lived in a scattered fashion and groups of no more than three or four grass huts were found (Irving, 1873, p. 300), although large numbers of Indians were seen in the same area during the salmon season (p. 444). Crawford met numbers of Indians along the Oregon Trail in southern Idaho in August, 1842 (Crawford, 1897, pp. 15-17) and in October of the following year Talbot observed of Indians near Shoshone Falls (1931, p. 53):

> These Indians speak the same language as the Snakes but are far poorer and are
> distinguished by the name of Shoshoccos, "Diggers," or "Uprooters." They have
> very few, and indeed most of them, have no horses....

Near Glenn's Ferry, however, Talbot met a large number of Indians of the "Waptico band of the Shoshonees," who had many horses (ibid., p. 55). Talbot drew the following conclusion from his experience on the Snake River (p. 56):

> It seems that there is a monopoly of the fisheries on the Snake River. The Banak Indians who are the most powerful, hold them in the spring when the salmon and other fishes are in best condition-later on different tribes of Shoshonees hord the monopoly. Last, and of course weakest of all, the miserable creatures such as are with us now, come, like gleaners after the harvest, to gather up the leavings of their richer and more powerful brethren.

Other sources contradict Talbot's observations, however, and give a picture of simultaneous use of the abundant salmon run by people of diverse locality and condition. But it is possible that mounted and more powerful people occupied the choicest sites.

During the late 1850's, the hostilities that broke out throughout Utah and Idaho also affected the Snake River. Wallen reported Indians peacefully fishing at Shoshone Falls in 1859, but commented that the Bannock upstream were well armed and formidable (Wallen, 1859, pp. 220, 223). In the same year. Will Wagner met on Goose Creek "several men of the band under the chief Ne-met-tek" (Wagner, 1861, p. 25) and encountered both Shoshone and Bannock in the high country between the Humboldt and Snake rivers (p. 26). Not all the Indians met exhibited hostile intentions in 1859 or in 1862 and 1863, when punitive forces were sent against the hostiles. Colonel Maury noted that "those perhaps who are more hostile are near Salmon Falls, or on the south side of Snake River" (War of the Rebellion, 1902, p. 217). Actually the hostiles were raiding along the Oregon Trail south of the Snake River, and it is probable that many of the peaceful Indians encountered also indulged in occasional attacks when in the neighborhood of the whites. Seventeen lodges and about 200 Indians were found near Shoshone Falls in August, 1863; these people reported that "the bad Indians are all gone to the buffalo country" (ibid, p. 218).

Further information from the military forces indicates a continuation of the older nomadic patterns. Colonel Maury said of Camas Prairie (ibid., p. 226):

> All the Indians living northwest of Salt Lake visit the grounds in the spring and summer, putting up their winter supply of camas, and after the root season is over, resort to the falls and other points on the Snake to put up fish.

In October, 1863, after the mounted people had left the fishing sites, Colonel Maury reported on the population along the Snake River (ibid., p. 224):

> They live a family in a place, on either side of the river for a distance of thirty or forty miles; have no arms and a very small number of Indian ponies; not an average of one to each family....There are from 80 to 100 of this party, all Shoshones, and, aware of the treaties made at Salt Lake, scattered along the river from the great falls to the mouth of this stream [the Bruneau River], a distance of 100 miles.

A party of 20 Indians was attacked by the military on the Bruneau River and there were signs in the upper part of the valley of a large force. Maury commented: "All the roaming Indians of the country visit the Bruneau River more or less." Further evidence of the mobility of the population is given in the report of attacks in the vicinity of Salmon Falls Creek by Indians from the Owyhee River under a medicine man named Ebigon (ibid., p. 388).

With the cessation of hostilities, most of the Shoshone and Bannock of Idaho were rapidly rounded up by the military and a few years later were settled at Fort Hall. Governor Lyon reported visiting the "great Kammas Prairie tribe of Indians" in 1865 (Lyon, 1867, p. 418), and Commissioner of Indian Affairs Cooley described the latter's territory as the "area around Fort Hall and the northern part of Utah" (Cooley, 1866, p. 198). Evidently the Indians who congregated annually at Camas Prairie were mistaken as a single tribe, and there is little further reference to such a group.

While it is almost impossible to identify Indians in the southwest Idaho region, west of the Bruneau River, Ballard's 1866 report of a mixed Paiute and Shoshone population probably represents the real situation (1867, p. 190).

> The southwest portion of Idaho, including the Owyhee country and the regions of the Malheur, are infested with a roving band of hostile Pi-utes and outlawed Shoshones, numbering, from the best information, some 300 warriors.

The reports of Indian Agents already cited in the section on the Boise River region indicate that the Bruneau River population was Shoshone. Their numbers are given as 400 in 1866 (ibid.) and 300 in 1868, after they had been brought to the Boise River (C. F. Powell, 1869, p. 661).

The frequent mention of a band of Bruneau Shoshone in the later reports of the Indian agents is somewhat misleading. Information from contemporary informants indicates that there was no distinct and separate population of the Bruneau River, as opposed to near-by stretches of the Snake River. Furthermore, the fisheries of the Bruneau River were often used by mounted Indians from the Fort Hall prairies.

There were no boundaries, as such, in southwest Idaho. Stewart's Tagotoka band of Northern Paiute is represented as occupying most of southwestern Idaho (Stewart, 1939, map 1, facing p. 127), while Blythe's equivalent "Tagu Eaters" are placed in the Owyhee River Valley (Blythe, 1938, p. 404). Blythe notes that east of this population there were "no pure Paiute bands." Steward's map places the limit between the Paiute and the Shoshone about equidistant between the Owyhee and Bruneau Rivers (Steward, 1938, fig. 1, facing p. ix). There was no hard and fast line between Shoshone and Paiute, and the high country south of Snake River was usually entered only in the summer when hunting parties of either linguistic group wandered through southwest Idaho. Further information the pattern of occupation of the Snake River and southwestern Idaho is given in the following ethnographic material.

Despite the extent of the region in question, there were not many permanent, or winter-dwelling, inhabitants. Greater use was made of the natural products of this region by the more numerous Shoshone and Bannock, who wintered elsewhere, than by the small local population. The two chief resources were the extremely rich root grounds at Camas Prairie, in the vicinity of Fairfield, Idaho, and the fishing sites scattered between Glenn's Ferry and Shoshone Falls. Camas Prairie was used by the Bannock and, to varying degrees, by all the Shoshone of Idaho, as well as occasionally by other tribes, like the Flathead and the Nez Percé; the fisheries were used by the Bannock and all the Shoshone of the upper Snake River above Shoshone Falls, the limit of the salmon run.

Some large stretches of territory were used very little, if at all. We were unable to obtain information on use or occupancy of the country north of the Snake River and south of the Sawtooths between Camas Prairie and Idaho Falls. This is extremely arid and infertile country, strewn with lava beds and containing little water. It was often traversed, but little subsistence was drawn from it. Also, scanty information was available on the territory west of the Bruneau River. One informant said that Silver City, Idaho, was within the limits of Paiute territory; according to other informants, the Bruneau River Valley was definitely within the Shoshone migratory range. It seems evident that southwest Idaho was not much used by either the Paiute or Shoshone, and, while both groups entered the area on occasion, boundaries could hardly have been narrowly defined.

The population which wintered in the general area of the middle Snake River and drew year-round subsistence from the resources of the region was usually referred to by the term Taza agaidika, or "Summer Salmon Eaters." Other terms used were Yahandika, or "Ground-hog Eaters," and Pia agaidika, or "Big Salmon Eaters." Steward reports the use of the terms Agaidüka and Yahandüka for the area (Steward, 1938, p. 165). One informant said that these were alternate terms which, however, did not change with the season or activities of the people designated. Lowie's Kuembedüka (Lowie, 1909, pp. 206-208) were not reported by our informants. Apparently, the names covered any and all people who wintered in the region and who were more or less permanent residents. The population included in these terms did not form a social or political group, nor did they unite for any collective purposes.

The Shoshone of the middle Snake River resemble the Nevada Shoshone in social, political, and economic characteristics more than does any other part of the Idaho population, and Steward lists them with the Western Shoshone for this reason. They had few horses and took no part in the buffalo-hunting activities of their neighbors of the Fort Hall plains, and warfare was virtually nonexistent. Property in natural resources was absent, and other Shoshone and the Bannock availed themselves freely of the fishing sites on the Snake River without interference or resentment on the part of the local population.

While chiefs are reported from most parts of Idaho, we were unable to obtain the name of a leader from the middle Snake River. Not only were there no band chiefs, but the winter villages lacked headmen. The principal informant for the area merely commented that everybody was equal.

Especially pronounced among the Shoshone of this area is the practice of splitting into a number of scattered and very small winter camps. Among the winter camps were: Akongdimudza, a camp at King Hill, Idaho, named for a hill which abounded in sunflowers; Biësoniogwe, a winter camp near Glenn's Ferry; Koa agai, near the hamlet of Hot Spring, Idaho, on the Bruneau River; and Paguiyua, a camp on Clover Creek near a hot spring, immediately up the Snake River from the town of Bliss, Idaho.

Winter camps were commonly located on the Snake River bottoms, where there was wood and shelter. The camps consisted of two or three lodges, each of which housed a family and a few relatives. The list of winter camps above is by no means complete; Steward gives three, two of which were below the town of Hagerman, a third near Bliss (Steward, 1938, pp. 165-166). There were undoubtedly several more, but it should be remembered that the place names above referred to sites which were not necessarily inhabited every winter.

The composition of the winter camps varied. While it was common for kinsmen to camp together, they by no means always did so. Also, the same people did not camp together every winter. Each family head decided each year where to spend the winter, and families were free to shift from one site to another annually. Steward's data confirm this practice (ibid., p. 169):

> ... it is apparent that the true political unit was the village, a small and probably unstable group. Virtually the only factor besides intervillage marriage that allied several villages was dancing. Dances, however, were so infrequent and the participants so variable that they produced no real unity in any group.

The Shoshone of the middle Snake River relied heavily on the salmon runs for food and fished during spring, summer, and fall. One fish weir, maintained on the Bruneau River, was frequently visited by Fort Hall Bannock, with whom the catch was shared. Glenn's Ferry was one of the better fishing sites; the waters between the three islands in the Snake River at this point were shallow enough for weirs to be used. Immediately above Hagerman, on the Snake River, the Indians caught salmon by spearing, although the water was too deep for weirs. Basketry traps were used in small creeks.

The Shoshone of this area took part in root gathering and festivities every summer on Camas Prairie. During the fall, deer were taken on Camas Prairie and in the country immediately south of the Snake River. Deer and elk were taken in the fall in the mountain country north of Hailey, and bighorn sheep were also pursued in the mountainous crags of this area.

In the great expanse of territory between Shoshone Falls and Bannock Creek only one small group is reported. These people were referred to as Paraguitsi, a word denoting the budding willow tree, and were said to inhabit Goose Creek and vicinity. Goose Creek is above the limit of the salmon run and only trout could be caught in its waters. Whether they fished below Shoshone Falls is uncertain. The area of the Goose Creek Mountains was entered also by people who wintered in other sections and was a frequent resort of Idaho and Nevada Shoshone in search of pine nuts.

Informants agreed that the Paraguitsi were a wild and timid people who remained isolated in the fastnesses of Goose Creek and the Goose Creek Mountains. This range provided them with deer and pine nuts, but their economy was meager and they were reported to resort to cannibalism in the winter. Other Shoshone avoided them because of this abhorrent practice.

One informant reported a category of "Mountain Dwellers," or Toyarivia. This was evidently a generic term for mountaineers as opposed to those who dwell in valleys, or Yewawgone. The Mountain Dwellers customarily spent the winter on the Snake River bottoms in the same area as the people generally called Taza agaidika. They joined in the salmon fishing at Glenn's Ferry and above, but hunted in the highlands on the Idaho-Nevada border during the fall. This division of mountain and valley people seems thus to have been occasionally used to distinguish Shoshone who hunted south of the Snake River from those who roamed to the north.

THE SHOSHONE OF THE SAWTOOTH MOUNTAINS

All informants agreed that the Sawtooth Mountains west of the Lemhi River and south of the Salmon River were inhabited by a Shoshone population designated as Tukurika (Dukarika and other variants). No Tukurika, or "Sheepeater," informants were interviewed on the Fort Hall Reservation, and we obtained only fragmentary information from Lemhi Shoshone and other Idaho Shoshone and Bannock.

Historical information on the Sheepeaters is scanty and mostly concerned with later periods. The earliest reference available comes from Ferris' journals. The Ferris party was in the Sawtooth Mountains, probably in or near Stanley Basin, in July, 1831. Ferris wrote (1940, p. 99):

> Here we found a party of "Root Diggers," or Snake Indians without horses. They subsist upon the flesh of elk, deer and bighorns, and upon salmon which ascend to the fountain sources of this river, and are here taken in great numbers....We found them extremely anxious to exchange salmon for buffalo meat, of which they are very fond, and which they never procure in this country, unless by purchase from their friends who occasionally come from the plains to trade with them.

The Stanley Basin region, it will be remembered, was a fall hunting range of the Shoshone of Boise River and was probably entered by others from Snake River. But as this was salmon season on both the Boise and Snake rivers, it is probable that Indians mentioned by Ferris were part of the more permanent population of the Sawtooths, i.e., Sheepeaters. The southern Sawtooths were no doubt utilized, like so many of our other areas, by people who customarily wintered in diverse places.

In June, 1832, John Work met "a party of Snakes consisting of three men and three women" near Meadow Creek on the Salmon River waters (Work, 1923, p. 160). Later references to the Sheepeaters indicate that they impinged upon the Shoshone of the Boise River on the west and the Lemhi on the east. Indian Agent Hough reported from the Boise River in 1868: "The Sheep Eaters have also behaved quite well; they are more isolated from the settlement, occupy a more sterile country, and are exceedingly poor" (Hough, 1869, p. 660). The Sheepeaters seem to have had their closest affiliations with the Shoshone of the Lemhi River, however, and they eventually moved to the agency founded there (Viall, 1872, p. 831; Shanks et al., 1874, p. 2).

The Tukurika were not a single group, but consisted of scattered little hunting groups having no over-all political unity or internal band organization. They had few horses and hunted mountain sheep and deer on foot. Salmon were taken in the waters of the Salmon River. The Tukurika had their closest contacts with the Lemhi Shoshone, although some occasionally visited the valleys of the Boise and Weiser rivers. I have no evidence of Tukurika trips to Camas Prairie for roots, although such visits are indicated by Steward's map (Steward, 1938, p. 136).

Steward lists five winter villages in the Sawtooth Mountains (ibid., pp. 188-189). These are:

1. Pasasigwana: This is the largest of the winter villages. It consisted of thirty families under the leadership of a headman who acted as director of salmon-fishing activities on the Salmon River. In the summer, the thirty families split into small groups and hunted on the Salmon River and its East Fork and in the Lost River and Salmon ranges. Steward reports that they obtained horses during a trip to Camas Prairie and thereafter joined the buffalo hunt. The village was situated north of Clayton.

2. Sohodai: Steward places this small village of six families on the upper reaches of the Middle Fork of the Salmon River.

3. Bohodai: This, the second largest Tukurika village, was on the Middle Fork of the Salmon near its confluence with the Salmon.

4. Another winter village was on the upper Salmon River and was merely an alternate camp for people who ordinarily wintered in Sohodai.

5. Pasimadai: This village, consisting of only two families, was on the upper Salmon River. It is the only one of the five listed that had no headman, although in another context Steward says (p. 193) that formal village chiefs were lacking before the consolidation with the Lemhi people.

The distribution of the Shoshone of the Sawtooth Mountains demarcates the northern limits of the Shoshone range. Steward's map of villages and subsistence areas in Idaho places the Shoshone on the Salmon River and the Middle Fork of the Salmon, while the lower parts of the Salmon River, below its junction with the South Fork, are assigned to the Nez Percé (p. 136). In his general map of the Basin-Plateau area (ibid., fig. 1, facing p. ix), Steward extends the Shoshone zone to the east side of Lost Trail Pass in Montana.

The data above represent substantial agreement with our own findings. Moving from west to east, the Snake River north of its junction with the Powder River (Oregon) is in precipitous canyon country and was no doubt little used. Mixed Shoshone and Mono-Bannock-speaking groups occupied the lower part of the Weiser River, but, as has been here stated, traded with the Nez Percé in the upper part of the valley. Some of the action of the Sheepeaters' War of 1878 took place in the mountains between the middle and south forks of the Salmon River, and there is no evidence of Shoshone use of the country north of the Salmon River. However, other groups apparently reached the Salmon River and its southern tributaries. Ferris met a village of Nez Percé on the Lemhi River in October, 1831 (Ferris, 1940, p. 120), and Wyeth reported a Nez Percé camp on the Salmon River in May 1833 (Wyeth, 1899, p. 194). The Nez Percé were also reported camped on Salmon River waters only one day from Fort Hall in August, 1839 (Farnham, 1906, p. 29). In the northeast corner of the area in question, Lewis and Clark first met the Flathead on the far side of Lost Trail Pass near present-day Sula, Montana, in August, 1805 (Lewis and Clark, 1904-06, 3:52). Shoshone no doubt crossed the pass occasionally and hunted there also, but this encounter and those reported in the preceding references indicate that the northern region of Shoshone nomadic activities was an area frequently entered and used by other peoples. Again, there is no strict boundary, but a zone of interpenetration.

THE SHOSHONE OF BANNOCK CREEK AND NORTHERN UTAH

There is little historic information on the specific area of Bannock Creek, Idaho. Almost all references to those Shoshone who were later found to have ranged through the area during part of the year is under the heading of Pocatello's band. This band was a hostile group under Chief Pocatello that raided white settlers and emigrants in the late 1850's and early 1860's. Pocatello's followers were mentioned along many points on the Oregon Trail through southern Idaho and were just as frequently reported in Box Elder and Cache counties in northern Utah.

The Fort Hall Indian Reservation is today effectively divided into two parts by the Portneuf River and the city of Pocatello. Most of the population, including the descendents of the Bannock and of the Lemhi, Fort Hall, Boise-Weiser, and Snake River Shoshone, live on the larger and more fertile northeastern section. On the southwestern half live many Shoshone Indians from northern Utah and from the area of Bannock Creek, which runs through this part of the reservation. The two populations mix to only a limited degree; each holds its own Sun Dance, and the people of the northern part of the reservation feel a true difference between themselves and those of the southern half. This separateness evidently goes back to pre-reservation times. The Bannock Creek Shoshone did not merge or interact very closely with the Shoshone of Fort Hall, and Bannock informants claim that they never had much to do with the latter.

The Bannock Creek Shoshone, as they are often called today, have been assigned a number of names. The most common, and the one most frequently used, is Hukandika or, as Hoebel transcribes it, Hᶾ'kandika (Hoebel, 1938, p. 410). Steward also reported this name for the Bannock Creek people, but since the Shoshone of Promontory Point were also so designated, Steward uses the alternate food name of Kumuduka, or "jackrabbit eaters," for the residents of Bannock Creek (Steward, 1938, p. 217). Other names are Yahandika (also applied to the salmon-fishing population of the middle Snake River), Yambarika ("yamp-root eaters"), and Sonivedika ("wheat eaters"). This last term is, of course, post-white and illustrates the adaptability of these names. Hukandika, or variants thereof, were reported in earlier times, although as a group living in northern Utah. Dunn wrote of the "Ho-kan-di-ka" of the Salt Lake Valley and Bear River (Dunn, 1886, p. 277), and Lander reported the "Ho-kanti'-kara, or Diggers on Salt Lake, Utah" (Wheeler, 1875, p. 409). For purposes of convenience, we shall refer to these Indians in this report as Bannock Creek Shoshone, although the range of their activities extended to the south well beyond this valley and into Utah.

More than any other Shoshone group in Idaho, the Bannock Creek people developed in the immediate post-contact period all the characteristics of the "predatory band," familiar to us from the Oregon Paiute and the Nevada Shoshone. The "predatory band" as illustrated among the latter population and among certain Ute and Nevada Shoshone groups, was a response to contact with the whites. The aborigines saw the sources of their subsistence threatened and were forced to defend themselves against the whites. Through trade and hostilities they acquired horses and thereby achieved the increased mobility and ease of communication necessary to a centrally led band organization. Plunder from wagon trains and ranches opened up new sources of wealth to them and made warfare attractive, over and above the needs of self defense. But always the nucleating force behind the bands was warfare and the prestige of certain war leaders.

The war leader of the Bannock Creek Shoshone was Pocatello, a name given him by the whites. Pocatello's band was listed among the "Western Snakes" by Lander in 1860: "Po-ca-ta-ra's band. Goose Creek Mountains, head of Humboldt, Raft Creek, and Mormon settlements horses few" (Lander, 1860, p. 137). Pocatello was also one of the signers of a treaty with Governor Doty at Box Elder on July 30, 1863; this treaty was an aftermath of General Connor's slaughter of the Shoshone on Bear River in January of the same year (Doty, 1865, p. 319). There was very little difficulty with the band after the Bear River battle. Superintendent Irish wrote in 1865 (1866, p. 311):

There are three bands of Indians known as the northwestern bands of the Shoshonees, commanded by three chiefs, Pocatello, Black Beard, and San Pitch, not under
the control of Wash-a-kee; they are very poor and number about fifteen hundred;
they range through the Bear River lake, Cache and Malade valleys, and Goose Creek
mountains, Idaho Territory.

Superintendent Head's report of 1866, however, indicates a continuing relation between the
Indians of southern Idaho and northern Utah and those of Wyoming (Head, 1867, p. 123).

A considerable number of these Indians [those of northern Utah and southern
Idaho known as Northwestern Shoshone after the treaty of 1863], including the
two chiefs Pokatello and Black Beard, have this season accompanied Washakee to
the Wind River valley on his annual buffalo hunt.

In the following year, Head summarized the distribution of mixed groups of Shoshone and
Bannock in the region (1868, p. 176).

They inhabit, during about six months in each year, the valleys of the Ogden,
Weber, and Bear rivers, in this territory. A considerable portion of their numbers remain there also during the whole year, while others accompany the Eastern
Shoshone to the Wind River valley to hunt buffalo. They claim as their country
also a portion of southern Idaho, and often visit that region, but game being there
scarce and the country mostly barren, their favorite haunts are as before stated.

According to Steward, Pocatello's band was an innovation in Bannock Creek (1938, p. 217):

Apparently there were several independent villages in this district in aboriginal days,
but when the people acquired many horses and the white man entered the country they began to consolidate under Pocatello, whose authority was extended over
people at Goose Creek to the west and probably at Grouse Creek [Utah].

Actual war parties were led by Pocatello and numbered only ten to twenty men, according
to one informant. Hostile activities were conducted especially on the Oregon Trail, which ran
through southern Idaho, and his band was responsible also for the attack at Massacre Rocks
(near the Snake River) and for various raids in northern Utah.

When not on the warpath, the Bannock Creek Shoshone followed a more prosaic round of
native subsistence activities. Information on the winter quarters of the Bannock Creek people
is uncertain. There were some winter camps on Bannock Creek, and one informant reported
that Pocatello also wintered on the Portneuf River between Pocatello and McCammon. Others
said that Pocatello wintered at times on the Bear River near the Utah-Idaho line.

Pocatello was not the only chief among the Bannock Creek people. Two others were named
Pete and Tom Pocatello, although their relation to Pocatello himself was doubtful. These chiefs
had their own followers, who were nonetheless known as Hukandika by informants. Tom
Pocatello remained in the general area of Malade City, Idaho, and Washakie, Utah, and wintered on the Bear River.

When they were not engaged in or threatened by hostilities, the Bannock Creek Shoshone
split into small camp groups much as they did in pre-white days. At least part of the band went
to Glenn's Ferry on the Snake River in the springtime, where they remained throughout the
salmon run. Similarly, many went-probably as individual families and camp groups-to Camas
Prairie for summer root digging. Others might travel into the Bear River and Bear Lake country,
while still others journeyed to Nevada to visit or to be present for the September pine-nut
harvests. Those who were mounted even traveled into Wyoming and visited and hunted buffalo
with the Eastern Shoshone.

With the previously mentioned Paraguitsi, the Bannock Creek people were the only Idaho Shoshone who depended upon the pine nut for an important part of their winter's provisions. These nuts could be obtained in the Goose Creek and Grouse Creek Mountains in late September. One informant reported that, if the harvest failed, many people went into the mountains west of Wendover and Ibapah, Utah, for the gathering there. A family could gather sufficient pine nuts in the fall, it was claimed, to last it until March.

The general round of migrations of the Bannock Creek people brought them into contact with the Shoshone of Nevada and with the small and scattered Shoshone groups of northern Utah, from whom they are almost indistinguishable. Buffalo hunting and common use of the Bear River region resulted in considerable interaction with the Eastern Shoshone, who also made use of this area in pre-reservation times. There was extensive intermarriage between the Eastern Shoshone and those of Bannock Creek and northern Utah, and one informant reports that their dialects were much alike. This affinity between the two groups finds further documentation in the belief of one of Steward's informants that the Bannock Creek people must have come from Wyoming (Steward, 1938, p. 217).

FORT HALL BANNOCK AND SHOSHONE

Above American Falls, the native population consisted of both Shoshone and Bannock Indians who were mounted and seasonally pursued the buffalo. Population aggregations were, in general, considerably larger than in any of the foregoing areas of Idaho. Ogden saw a "Snake" camp of 300 tents, 1,300 people and 3,000 horses on Little Lost River in November, 1827 (Ogden, 1910, p. 364), and Beckwourth claimed that he had met thousands of mounted and hostile Indians at the mouth of the Portneuf River in the spring of 1826 (Beckwourth, 1931, pp. 64-65).

The journal of Warren Angus Ferris contains many references to the population in eastern Idaho in the period 1831-1833. The area evidently was frequently entered by warlike Blackfoot parties and by more peaceful groups of Flathead, Nez Percé, and Pend Oreille trappers and buffalo hunters (cf. Ferris, 1940, pp. 87, 146, 153-155, 185). Buffalo were still to be found and Ferris encountered large herds on the upper Snake River (ibid., p. 87); Nez Percé and Flathead Indians were seen on the divide between Birch Creek and the Lemhi River en route to hunt buffalo (ibid., p. 146). But the Indians most frequently encountered in the region were Bannock and Shoshone. On the Snake River plains near Three Buttes Ferris noted (p. 132):

> In the evening two hundred Indians passed our camp, on their way to the village, which was situated at the lower butte. They were Ponacks, as they are generally called by the hunters, or Po-nah-ke as they call themselves. They were generally mounted on poor jaded horses, and were illy clad.

In November, 1832, it was reported that "a village of Snakes and Ponacks amounting to about two hundred lodges on Gordiez [Big Lost] River" was attacked by a party of Blackfoot (ibid., pp. 185-186). The "Snakes" drove them off, but the "Horn Chief" was killed. The Horn Chief was reported on the Bear River in 1830 (ibid., pp. 71-73). This group may have been the same one mentioned a month later as being in winter camp on the Portneuf River (ibid., p. 188). Another Bannock camp was found in December, 1832, on the Blackfoot River. Ferris wrote (ibid., pp. 189-190):

> I visited their village on the 20th and found these miserable wretches to the number of eighty or one hundred families, half-naked, and without lodges, except in one or two instances. They had formed, however, little huts of sage roots, which were yet so open and ill calculated to shield them from the extreme cold, that I could not conceive how they were able to endure such severe exposure.

Ferris' description does not seem typical of the Plainslike Bannock Indians. There are two possible explanations: these Bannock had been attacked by hostiles and had lost their possessions; or they had recently moved westward from Oregon. The latter possibility cannot be ruled out, for the Bannock and the Northern Paiute were in contact during the salmon season and the Oregon people drifted over to join their colinguists on the upper Snake River until much later in the century.

The presence of the Horn Chief on the Big Lost River in Idaho and the Bear River in Utah bespeaks the fact that the residents of eastern Idaho entered the northern Utah region quite as frequently as did the Shoshone of western Wyoming. Zenas Leonard reported meeting Bannock Indians some four days' travel west of the Green River. Depending on their speed, the trappers may have been in southern Idaho or some part of northern Utah. Leonard wrote of the Bannock (1934, p. 105):

> On the fourth day of our Journey we arrived at the huts of some Bawnack Indians. These Indians appear to live very poor and in the most forlorn condition. They generally make but one visit to the buffaloe country during the year, where they remain until they jerk as much meat as their females can lug home on their backs. They then quit the mountains and return to the plains where they subsist on fish

and small game the remainder of the year. They keep no horses and are always easy prey for other Indians provided with guns and horses.

It would be difficult to imagine a people without horses traveling across the Continental Divide for buffalo, and it must be assumed that the near-by herds that then existed were used.

Bonneville met a Bannock winter camp in January, 1833, near the Snake River, in the vicinity of Three Buttes (Irving, 1850, p. 88). They numbered 120 lodges and were said to be deadly enemies of the Blackfoot, whom they easily overcame when their forces were equal. In the following winter the Bannock camp was at the mouth of the Portneuf River, near the last season's site (Irving, 1837, 2:41). And in August, 1834, Townsend saw two lodges of some twenty "Snakes" who were "returning from the fisheries and traveling towards the buffalo on the 'big river' (Shoshone's) [Snake River]" (Townsend, 1905, p. 245).

Russell's journal provides further description of buffalo hunting on the upper Snake River. He himself hunted buffalo out of the newly established Fort Hall post in 1834 (Russell, 1955, pp. 7-8). On October 1 of that year a village of 60 lodges of "Snakes" was found on Blackfoot River; the chief was "Iron wristbands" or "Pah-da-her-wak-un-dah." On October 20 a camp of 250 "Bonnak" lodges arrived at Fort Hall. Russell met some 332 lodges, of six persons each, hunting buffalo in the vicinity of Birch Creek in October, 1835 (p. 36). Their chief was "Aiken-lo-ruckkup," a brother of the late Horn Chief. The trapper also found 15 lodges of "Snakes" in the same area (p. 37). Twenty-five miles east of the Bannock camp, Russell found a buffalo-hunting camp of 15 "Snake" lodges under "Chief Comb Daughter," or the "Lame Chief" (p. 38). Presumably, Russell's "Snakes" were Shoshone. The buffalo evidently disappeared from the Snake River drainage by 1840, for the last reference to their presence in this region is in January, 1839, when Russell mentions the presence of buffalo bulls on the upper Snake River (p. 93).

Lieutenant John Mullan encountered two "Banax" Indians in December, 1853, on the Jefferson River in Montana. They had crossed the mountains from the Salmon River country in hopes of meeting other Bannock returning from the buffalo hunt. He noted the inroads on their numbers made by smallpox and the Blackfoot and commented (Mullan, 1855, p. 329. "The most of them now inhabit the country near the Salmon River, where, in their solitude and security, they live perfectly contented in spearing the salmon, and living on roots and berries.") Across the divide between Montana and Idaho, in the vicinity of Camas Creek, they met a single Bannock lodge en route to the mountains (p. 333). North of Fort Hall, the party came upon three or four families of "Root Digger Indians" whose destitute condition was described by Mullan (p. 334).

The Bannock had visited Fort Bridger for purposes of trade over a period of many years and continued the practice after the end of the fur boom. Superintendent Jacob Forney reported that some 500 Bannock under chief "Horn" appeared there in 1859 and claimed a home in the Utah Territory (Forney, 1860a, p. 31). Forney granted them permission to remain in the region claimed by Washakie. A body of Bannock was in the vicinity of Fort Bridger in 1867, but Washakie refused to share the Eastern Shoshone allotment with them. It will be remembered that a part of the Bannock population had been collected on the Boise River prior to this time. Indians denominated as Bannock were evidently to be found in a number of places during this period. Commissioner of Indian Affairs Taylor reported in 1868 (1869, p. 683):

> The other tribes in Montana are the Bannock and the Shoshones, ranging about
> the headwaters of the Yellowstone, and reported to be in a miserable and destitute
> condition. These Indians it is believed are parties to a treaty made by Gov. Doty on
> the 14th of Oct., 1863, at Soda Springs, not proclaimed. As they occupy a part of
> the country claimed by the Crows, I think it advisable ... to induce them to remove
> to the Shoshone country, in the valley of the Shoshone (Snake) River.

In the same year Mann assembled 800 Bannock for a treaty conference, but one-half of this number left the gathering in June, 1868, when the commissioner failed to appear (Mann, 1869,

p. 617). The 800 Bannock were gathered by Chief "Taggie" (Tygee), who was also mentioned in the 1869 report of the Fort Hall Agent (Danilson, 1870, p. 730).

Unless the Bannock were an amazingly mobile people, they must have traveled in a number of groups during the late 1860's. Superintendent Sully of Montana wrote in September, 1869 (Sully, 1870, p. 731):

> ... [the Bannock] are a very small tribe of Indians, not mustering over five hundred souls. They claim the southwestern portion of Montana as their land, containing some of the richest portions of the territory, in which are situated Virginia City, Boseman City, and many other places of note.

However, Superintendent Floyd-Jones of Idaho reported in 1869 (1870, p. 721):

> The Bannacks, about six hundred strong, have always claimed this country, and promise that this winter's hunt in the Wind River Mountains shall be their last...

Groups of Bannock were variously reported in Wyoming, Montana, and Idaho during these years, and it is to be assumed that they sought both buffalo and rations. Governor Campbell of Wyoming wrote in October, 1870, that the Bannock had spent the summer with the Crow Indians (J. A. Campbell, 1871, p. 639) after leaving Wind River. The Bannock were evidently the most difficult to settle of all the Idaho Indians, and their nomadic propensities were restrained only after the conclusion of the Bannock War of 1878. The data that follow were gathered through ethnographic means and continue and summarize the foregoing historical account.

The Bannock population of the Fort Hall plains was undoubtedly resident in that area for a considerable period. Living on the western slope of the Continental Divide, they crossed the mountains frequently to hunt in the buffalo country of the Missouri drainage. In the process they came into contact with tribes of the Plains and borrowed a good deal of culture from them. However, contact with the Paiute of Oregon continued. During the Bannock War of 1878 the Fort Hall insurgents were joined by the rebellious inmates of the Malheur Agency in eastern Oregon. Also, genealogies given by informants indicate that many Northern Paiute were still leaving their Oregon habitat as late as the time of the treaty and thereafter and were joining the Bannock in their more abundant and exciting life of warfare and buffalo hunting. In effect, these migrants became "Bannock" when they began to live with the Bannock. The formation of the Bannock in southeastern Idaho from Oregon Paiute who managed to get horses and were attracted by the buffalo hunt was not a single occurrence at some indefinite time in the past; it was a continuing process that lasted into the reservation period. There is no evidence placing the Bannock in the Fort Hall area before the introduction of the horse. It is doubtful that they predated this time, given the fact that buffalo hunting on horse was one of the main attractions of eastern Idaho.

The relation of the Bannock to neighboring Shoshone groups, denominated by the generic term, "Wihinait," is somewhat problematic and can best be understood from detailed consideration of the two populations. Steward says that "the Fort Hall Bannock and Shoshoni were probably comparatively well amalgamated into a band by 1840" (Steward, 1938, p. 202), but also notes (p. 10) that "Bannock and Shoshoni, though closely cooperating and living on terms of equality, were politically distinct in that each had its band chief." Our evidence indicates that there was a good deal of social intercourse and intermarriage and coöperation in the buffalo hunt between the two groups, but except when engaged in some joint endeavor each appears to have maintained its autonomy. Although there were organized bands, their lines were not very clear-cut because of their frequent fission (ibid., p. 202):

> Even with the advantage of the horse, it was not always expedient for the combined Bannock-Shoshoni band to move as a unit. They frequently split into small subdivisions, each of which travelled independently through Southern Idaho to procure different foods, to trade, and occasionally to carry on warfare.

Despite the presence of many Plains Indian culture elements, the social structure of the Fort Hall people was basically that of the Shoshonean population of the Basin-Plateau. While they grouped into larger units for certain defined purposes, these units functioned only during part of the year. The internal organization of the bands was fluid, amorphous, and shifting.

The question of the constitution of the bands also remains: was there one large Fort Hall Shoshone and Bannock band, were there one Fort Hall Bannock and one Fort Hall Shoshone band, or were both populations split into smaller groups? Both Steward and Hoebel reject the first possibility, and the answer seems to lie somewhere between the second and third. Hoebel names four Bannock bands (1938, p. 412): Cottonwood Salmon Eaters, Deer Eaters, Squirrel Eaters, Plant (?) Eaters. One informant told us also of four food names among the Bannock. These were: Biviadzugarika ("root [?] eaters,") Topihabirika ("root [?] eaters"), Tohocharika ("deer eaters"), and Yaparika ("yamp eaters"). Only part of the Fort Hall Bannock population bore these names. The names did not refer to band groupings of any type, and their bearers were of various bands. Our informant did not know the origin of this nomenclature. It is possible that the names designated Oregon food areas and were applied to more recent migrants from the Oregon Paiute, but the names do not bear sufficiently close correspondence to those given by Blythe and Stewart to validate this assumption.

Bannock informants claimed that there was a head chief of all the Bannock, Tahgee, and that subchiefs under him were leaders of smaller groups at certain times of the year. The subchiefs were said to have attended the treaty conference at Fort Bridger with Tahgee. Their names were Patsagumudu Po'a, Kusagai, Totowa, Pagoit, and Tahee. Tahgee represented the Bannock in their affairs with the whites and was the leader of the buffalo hunt. Otherwise, he seems to have exerted little direct authority over his people, although he had great influence in council. Bannock informants all asserted that people went where they wished when they wished and did not necessarily travel under any form of leadership.

Bannock chieftainship was nonhereditary and was assigned by general agreement to a man noted for wisdom and courage.

Among the Shoshone of the Fort Hall region, leadership was more clearly a function of inter-action with the whites. One man was said to have become chief "because he helped the whites." Two chiefs were reported, Aidamo and Aramun; the bands of both roamed through southeast-ern Idaho and into northern Utah. These Shoshone were called by the Bannock, "Winakwat," or "Wihinait" in Shoshone. The name evidently did not refer to a single band but designated all Shoshone-speaking people of the immediate area. I could find no confirmation of Hoebel's Elk Eaters, Groundhog Eaters, and Minnow Eaters, all of whom were said to live in the area roamed over by the various Fort Hall Shoshone and Bannock groups (Hoebel, 1938, pp. 410-413).

In the Fort Hall area, as in the rest of Idaho, winter habitat supplies the only stable crite-rion for identifying the several groups or populations. The Bannock customarily wintered on the Snake River bottoms above Idaho Falls and at the mouth of Henry's Fork near Rexburg, Idaho. They also wintered downstream in the vicinity of the modern town of Blackfoot, Idaho; historical sources mention Bannock winter camps at the mouth of the Portneuf River. The Snake River-Henry's Fork sites were favored because of the abundance of the mule-tailed deer, which came into the bottomlands in the winter. Another source of subsistence in winter was cottontail rabbits, which were caught among the willows in the bottoms with a noose snare or by surrounding them and killing them with the bow and arrow.

The main winter subsistence, and the food source that provided the margin of survival, was the dried meat of buffalo, elk, and deer taken in the fall hunts, supplemented by dried roots and berries. Food caches were maintained near camp, but they were generally resorted to only in the spring, when the dried food kept in the lodges was exhausted. The location of the cache was known only to the family that made it. Caches and their contents were considered private property. Dried roots, berries, and salmon were generally kept in the underground caches, but not meat.

Bannock winter camps were spread out along the river; there was no central encampment. The population was predominantly Bannock, although many Shoshone lived among them either through in-marriage or by choice.

Not all of the Bannock wintered on the Snake River. Those who crossed the divide for buffalo frequently did not return in time to cross the mountains before the snows blocked the high passes and so generally wintered in western Montana, not joining the rest until spring.

The Wihinait, or Shoshone of the Fort Hall area, were said to have wintered apart from the Bannock on the Portneuf River. Winter camps ranged along the Portneuf between Pocatello and McCammon, and other places as far south as Malade City, Idaho, were sometimes occupied. Here, too, the population lived off stored food and whatever game could be taken.

The winter quarters of the Shoshone were more secure from enemy attack, however, than were those of the Bannock. The only hostile tribe to enter southern Idaho with any frequency was the Blackfoot. They pressed their attacks vigorously, especially against the Bannock, and were a subject of some wonder owing to their practice of sending out war parties in the middle of winter. Blackfoot war parties, consisting only of men, frequently came south from Montana before the passes were closed by the winter snows and made camp on Henry's Fork, near the present site of St. Anthony, Idaho. From this convenient point they sent small raiding parties against the Bannock camps. The main purpose of these raids was to capture horses, which were driven north to the Blackfoot country when the passes opened in the spring. Although the Bannock were kept on the defensive, they were not the helpless prey of the Blackfoot. Defensive tactics were frequently too late, for the enemy drove off horses surreptitiously by night, but counterraids were made and pursuit was given in return. The Blackfoot occasionally pressed their raids farther downstream and entered the Portneuf Valley, but such forays were less frequent. Historical records, however, mention Blackfoot raids in Yellowstone Park and Jackson Hole and as far south as the valleys of the Green and Bear rivers and Great Salt Lake.

When spring arrived the winter camp broke up and both Shoshone and Bannock split up into small groups, each of which went their separate ways. Hunting was the first undertaking after breaking up winter camp. The spring hunt was usually conducted in Idaho rather than in more distant places, since most people wished to return later in the spring for salmon fishing at Glenn's Ferry. Small parties of only a few lodges each roamed through the mountains of Caribou County, Idaho, in search of deer and elk, while others went southwards into the Bear River and Bear Lake country. Chub were caught in Bear River, and duck eggs were gathered and ducks killed in the marshes at the north end of Bear Lake. During the spring wanderings, roots were dug also.

The route to Bear River went through much the same country as modern U.S. Highway 30 N. Parties ascended the Portneuf River and crossed the divide to the Bear River at the site of Soda Springs. They continued south on the Bear River to Montpelier. Those who did not intend to return for salmon but wished to visit the Eastern Shoshone ascended the Bear River to Cokeville and Sage and crossed the Bear River Divide, passing the fossil-fish beds en route.

As has been mentioned, not all the Shoshone and Bannock went to Glenn's Ferry to take salmon; those who did went in small groups rather than in a body. Parties followed the Snake River down to Glenn's Ferry, where they fished with harpoons. The Fort Hall people apparently did not make fish weirs. The weirs were usually the work of the winter population of the salmon areas, but one informant stated that the Bannock shared in the catch.

Some Bannock continued downstream past Glenn's Ferry and fished in the Bruneau River, while others went to the Boise and Weiser rivers. Trade was conducted with the Nez Percé in the Weiser Valley; informants did not believe that the Bannock or the Shoshone took part in the trade with the Columbia River tribes in the Grand Ronde Valley in northeastern Oregon. This trade was, however, before the memories of any of our informants (or of their fathers).

At the conclusion of the spring salmon run, the scattered camp grounds of Fort Hall Shoshone and Bannock went to Camas Prairie, where they dug camas, yamp, and other roots and fattened their horses for the fall hunt. Roots could also be dug in other areas, like the Weiser Valley and the plains and foothills near Fort Hall, and some families did not go to Camas Prairie.

In most years Camas Prairie served as the marshalling grounds for the annual buffalo hunt. On these occasions, Bannock and mounted Shoshone of the Fort Hall area joined forces. While it is possible that these groups combined also with the Lemhi Shoshone for the buffalo hunt, we could obtain no corroboration of this grouping from informants. Informants generally stated that the buffalo party was composed chiefly of Bannock and was led by the Bannock chief. While many Fort Hall Shoshone took part, most hunted elk, moose, and deer on the western side of the Continental Divide. Furthermore, some Bannock did not take part in the hunt and similarly hunted in Idaho and southwestern Wyoming.

It should be noted that information on the entry of Shoshone or Bannock groups into the buffalo grounds of Montana occurs very early in the historical period in the reports of Lewis and Clark, and also very late in this period. It is true that there is little pertinent historical data on southwestern Montana, but there is a distinct possibility that the Shoshone and Bannock did not cross the Divide annually. Buffalo were found on the upper Snake River prairie until about 1840, and the presence of the Blackfoot in Montana made ventures there risky. It is noteworthy that in the early reservation period the Bannock crossed the Divide into the Big Horn drainage in company with the Eastern Shoshone; the trip through Green River and thus to Wind River was not by any means the shortest route to the buffalo country. On the other hand, informants gave highly detailed information on the trail to the Montana buffalo grounds and showed detailed traditional knowledge of it. Without more continuous historical data such as is available on transmontane hunting patterns in Wyoming, any question of historical changes in hunting itineraries must remain open.

From Camas Prairie, contemporary informants say, the buffalo party skirted the southern end of the Sawtooth Mountains and went up the Little Lost River, crossing over to the Lemhi River. They then traveled down the Lemhi and across the Divide via Lemhi Pass. Descending the east side of the mountains, the buffalo party arrived on the Beaverhead River at a point close to Armstead, Montana. They then traveled down the Beaverhead past Twin Bridges to the point where the Beaverhead becomes the Jefferson River and thence downstream to the Three Forks of the Missouri. One informant said that the Beaverhead Valley contained buffalo in earlier times, but by the period preceding the treaty it was necessary to go much farther east. From Three Forks, Montana, the buffalo route followed the present line of U.S. Highway 10 through Bozeman and over Bozeman Pass. The party pressed eastwards until it arrived in the country called Buffalo Heart by the Bannock because a near-by mountain supposedly had the shape of a buffalo heart; this was the fall and winter hunting grounds of the Idaho Shoshone and Bannock. It was near the Yellowstone River between Big Timber and Billings, Montana, though the migratory habits of buffalo and buffalo hunters would dictate considerable movement within the region.

The buffalo hunters remained to the west of the Bighorn River and, presumably, they did not encroach too heavily upon the Crow. While the Crow considered the Eastern Shoshone enemies, we have no information on hostilities between them and the Idaho people. The Bannock actually camped with the Crow in the late 1860's and early 1870's.

To return to the route to the buffalo country, some alternate trails must be noted. After leaving Camas Prairie the party sometimes passed through Arco and Idaho Falls, Idaho, and then headed north over the Divide, via Monida Pass. They followed Red Rock Creek down to its confluence with the Beaverhead and followed the previously described trail.

Also, the buffalo party did not always reach Bozeman Pass via the Three Forks of the Missouri. The alternate route crossed from the Beaverhead River to the Madison River via Virginia City. The party continued down the Madison a short distance and then went east to Bozeman where the trail joined the one already outlined. There were undoubtedly several other routes that are no longer remembered by informants.

The buffalo hunt was conducted by much the same techniques as already described for the Eastern Shoshone. Two scouts were sent out to report upon the presence of buffalo, and the party surrounded and pursued the herd as a group. No police societies to prevent hunting by individuals were reported by our Idaho Shoshone and Bannock informants, nor is there historic evidence of the institution. Guns, spears, and the bow and arrow were used.

Meat was jerked and dried on the plains and the slain buffalo were skinned and their hides dried. When as much of these commodities as the pack horses could carry was accumulated, the party struck out for home. Owing to the great distance between the Snake River Valley and the buffalo country, winter usually overtook the party en route. If the passes were still open when the hunters reached the Divide, they went into winter quarters on the Snake River. If the heavy snows caught the party while still far from the mountains, they kept traveling slowly westward and attempted to encamp in one of the well wooded and sheltered valleys on the east side of the Divide. When the passes opened in the spring, they crossed into Idaho.

During the winter the party subsisted upon the dried buffalo meat and whatever game could be killed. An important product of the hunt, the most important according to one informant, was the buffalo hides from which tipis and robes were made. Since there was no spring hunt and other game was plentiful in eastern Idaho and western Wyoming in the fall, the hides may well have been the primary attraction of the buffalo country.

Those Shoshone and Bannock who did not follow the buffalo party carried on the fall hunt in southeastern Idaho, northern Utah, and western Wyoming. The elk and deer hunted could best be taken by small groups, hence hunting parties were not large and communal techniques were not necessary. Also, since these animals were scattered throughout the region and did not travel in the huge herds characteristic of the buffalo, the population had to spread out accordingly. Somewhat larger groups gathered to hunt antelope, but these were temporary aggregations. The actual size of the fall hunting groups is uncertain. One informant said that each consisted of about fifteen tipis, while another said that groups of two to four tipis were common. These smaller camp groups were known as *nanogwa*. Their size was said to have made them more vulnerable to attack than the somewhat larger concentrations.

Some locales were known to have a plentiful supply of certain game animals. Caribou County in southeastern Idaho was considered good for deer hunting, while Jackson Hole and Yellowstone Park were noted for elk. The arid highlands of southwestern Wyoming abounded in antelope. Of course, all of these areas contained other types of game, and wild vegetables could be obtained in all.

The fall hunt began at the end of August or in early September when the game was growing fat. Some parties went from Camas Prairie to Jackson Hole and Yellowstone via Idaho Falls and the Snake River. The route used was much the same as that followed by U.S. Highway 26. One informant spoke of Targhee Pass and West Yellowstone, Idaho, as being a point of entry to and departure from the Yellowstone country. The Snake River Trail was more commonly used to enter Jackson and Yellowstone, although West Yellowstone seems to have been more frequently traveled on the homeward journey. The west slope of the Tetons, the area drained by Teton River, was used also by hunting parties.

Other Bannock and Shoshone camp groups went southward through the Portneuf Valley and over to the Bear River at Soda Springs; they followed the Bear River until they bore eastward to Kemmerer, Wyoming. Most camps of the Idaho Indians remained on the west side of the Green River. The chief game of the area was the antelope herds which were found on affluents of the Green River, northeast of Kemmerer. The Idaho Shoshone and Bannock were joined in the antelope hunt by the Eastern Shoshone of Wyoming and by the Ute, some of whom crossed the Uinta Range in early autumn for this purpose. Whether all these people actually combined for communal hunts is uncertain. It is more probable that small groups from each population amalgamated. Another attraction of the Green River country was Fort Bridger, where many of the Indians went for trade.

A few camps might remain to winter in the Green River country, but most of them continued their hunt in other parts while returning to winter quarters. Some camps retraced their outward route, but others traveled northward through Star Valley in western Wyoming and thence up the Snake River to Jackson Hole. It must be kept in mind that there was no central camp group nor were there fixed hunting trails that each group had to follow and that were recognized as their rightful grounds. Camp groups could travel where they pleased and when they pleased. Proprietary rights to hunting grounds were not recognized.

The individual camp groups changed in composition and membership annually. A small camp of only a few tipis might consist of consanguineally and affinally related people, but such association was not a fixed rule. Also, a family could leave one hunting group and join another at will.

The hunting season ended with the advent of winter. Camp groups drifted into the previously described winter quarters and awaited spring, when the cycle would begin again.

LEMHI SHOSHONE

One of the most cohesive of all Shoshone groups lived in the valley of the Lemhi River on the western slope of the Continental Divide. The Lemhi Shoshone were commonly known by the term Agaidika, or "salmon eaters." Like the people of the Fort Hall plains they had fairly large herds of horses, which enabled them to take part in the transmontane buffalo hunt.

Excellent data on the early historic period in Lemhi Valley is found in the journals of Lewis and Clark, who crossed the Continental Divide to the Lemhi River on August 13, 1805. A certain amount of information on the Shoshone penetration of Montana can be derived from this source. Sacajawea, the young Shoshone woman who acted as guide and interpreter for Lewis and Clark, said that she had been kidnaped during an attack upon the Shoshone at a camp at the Three Forks of the Missouri River (Lewis and Clark, 1804-06, 2:283). On their return journey from the Pacific the explorers passed through Big Hole Valley, slightly above the present town of Wisdom, Montana, where it was noted that they were "in the great plain where Shoshonees gather Quawmash and cows etc." (ibid., 5:250-251). The party proceeded westward up the Beaverhead River, where Sacajawea claimed the Shoshone were sometimes found (p. 321) and above Dillon saw one mounted Indian thought to be Shoshone (p. 329). No other Indians were sighted, although there were indications on the upper Beaverhead River that Indians had been digging roots (pp. 332, 334). Apparently the buffalo had been receding to the east even at that early time, for Sacajawea said that they used to come to the very head of the Beaverhead River; apparently they had been hunted out by the Shoshone, who tried to avoid the trip to the plains by killing as many buffalo as possible in the mountains (p. 261). It seems evident that the Indians' acquisition of the horse resulted in some depletion of the buffalo long before the American hide hunters arrived in the West.

The main body of Shoshone was encountered by Lewis and Clark on their westward trip in the Lemhi River Valley. The natives were fishing at the time, and their camps were found scattered along the stream. Camps of seven families and of one family (ibid., 3:6, 11), and another of 25 lodges (ibid., 2:175) serve as examples of the residence units met. Lewis estimated the population of the valley as 100 warriors and 300 women and children (ibid., p. 372). They possessed some 700 mounts, including 40 colts and 20 mules; this, it would seem, was not an adequate number for the needs of extensive buffalo hunting beyond the Continental Divide.

The social needs of buffalo hunting evidently produced some degree of band political integration among the Shoshone. But the "principal Chief," Ca-me-ah-wait (ibid., p. 340) had only limited powers. Lewis writes (ibid., p. 370):

> ...each individual is his own sovereign master, and acts from the dictates of his own mind; the authority of the Chief being nothing more than mere admonition supported by the influence which the propriety of his own exemplary conduct may have acquired him in the minds of the individuals who compose the band.

The title of chief was nonhereditary, and, in fact, everybody was to varying degrees a "chief," Lewis noted; the most influential of the men was recognized by the others as the "principal chief."

The Shoshone had been pushed westward by the incursions of Indian tribes armed by the Canadian traders. Ca-me-ah-wait told Lewis that the Shoshone would be able to remain on the Missouri waters if equipped with firearms, but under the circumstances had to live part of the year on the Columbia waters, where they ate only fish, roots, and berries (ibid., p. 383). A few Shoshone in the Lemhi Valley had firearms that they obtained from the Crow Indians of the Yellowstone River (ibid., p. 341). The winter quarters of the Lemhi Shoshone are not described in the journals, but Lewis wrote that they remained on the Columbia waters during the time of the salmon run, from May to September, and then crossed the Divide to the Missouri waters where they spent the winter (p. 373). The presence of powerful and hostile tribes in the buffalo country forced the Lemhi Shoshone to travel in numbers. They were joined by Shoshone from other areas in the Lemhi Valley and were reinforced by more Shoshone groups and the Flathead at the Three Forks of the Missouri (p. 324).

The Lemhi Shoshone were preparing to leave for the buffalo hunt on August 23, 1805. The salmon run was dwindling at the time of the explorers' visit, for Clark noted that the Indians were living largely on berries and roots and were quite hungry (ibid., p. 367). Antelope were hunted by horsemen pursuing the animals in relays, but it was observed that 40 to 50 men might spend a half-day in this activity and take only two or three antelope (ibid., p. 346).

The relations of the Shoshone with the outer world gives some indication of their pattern of movement. They ranged southward to the Spanish settlements, for some of their mules were obtained from the Spaniards and articles of Spanish manufacture were noted (ibid., p. 347). The Shoshone were already suffering from smallpox and venereal disease (ibid., p. 373).

Enemy tribes inflicted losses upon the Shoshone. The "Minetaree of Fort de prairie" had attacked them and stolen horses and tipis (ibid., p. 343), and they had but recently made peace with the Cayuse and Walla Walla (ibid., 5:157-158). The Nez Percé also had frequent clashes with the Shoshone (ibid., pp. 24, 55-56, 113); the territorial situation between the Shoshone and Nez Percé was evidently the same as in later times, for Ca-me-ah-wait stated that the Nez Percé lived on the Salmon River, "below the mountains" (ibid., 2:382). Friendly relations were maintained with the Flathead, who, according to the journals, lived on the Bitterroot River, but fished on the Salmon River (ibid., 3:22).

Later references to the Lemhi River region and adjacent portions of Montana are few. Ferris hunted on the Ruby River in Montana in the early fall of 1831 and mentioned no Shoshone. He did, however, meet a Nez Percé camp of 25 lodges (Ferris, 1940, p. 118). Another Nez Percé camp was encountered after Ferris crossed the Divide to the Lemhi River (ibid., p. 120). Ferris went to the Ruby River again in 1832 and again found no Shoshone. His party was attacked by the Blackfoot and the trappers found refuge in a camp on the Beaverhead River consisting of 150 lodges of "Flatheads, Pen-d'oreilles, and others" (ibid., pp. 177-178). In 1831, Ferris crossed over Deer Lodge Pass to Big Hole River, where he noted that they were on the edge of Blackfoot country (ibid, p. 109). However, he met 100 lodges of Pend Oreilles on Big Hole River who were en route from Salish House to the buffalo country. Ferris then joined the Pend Oreille and some Flathead lodges in a buffalo hunt on the Beaverhead River (ibid., p. 113).

An obvious conclusion from the preceding data is that the Shoshone did hunt in southwestern Montana, but so also did other peoples. The flux of various hunting parties in the area was undoubtedly increased during the fur-trapping period. The extent of their entry into Montana remains undetermined, but their range undoubtedly shifted during the historic period as a direct result of the recession eastward of the buffalo herds. It is uncertain what proportion of the Lemhi population went on the buffalo hunt, and we lack historical information on their winter camps across the Divide. However, casual entry of small parties into southwestern Montana for winter residence would have been most dangerous throughout the historic period because of the continual threat of Blackfoot attacks.

Leadership patterns were well developed among the Lemhi people. In 1859 Lander mentioned "Tentoi" who "is not a chief, but has very great influence with the tribe, and has distinguished himself in wars with the Blackfeet" (Lander, 1860, p. 125). Tendoy was subsequently said by Agent Rainsford to be the head chief at Lemhi (Rainsford, 1873, p. 666), and Agent Fuller later noted Tendoy as the chief of the entire reservation population, which included some 200 Bannock, 500 Shoshone, and 300 Sheepeaters (Fuller, CD 1639, p. 572). Further information on Tendoy was obtained from informants, but it is obvious that the establishment of a reservation in Lemhi Valley resulted in an eclectic population and the chieftaincy was part of the Indian Office pattern of reservation administration. There is no doubt, however, that a pre-reservation chieftaincy did exist, although for different purposes.

Informants agreed that the Agaidika formed a unified band under Tendoy. No other chiefs were named, although there were said to be a number of minor leaders. Tendoy acted as leader in such communal pursuits as the making of salmon traps or in the annual buffalo hunt. Informants said that he called a council of leading men of the band when any decision affecting the whole group was to be made, and the results were announced to the people by a man who held the office of "announcer." Councils might be held before the salmon season and the buffalo hunt or to plot strategy when on the buffalo hunt.

While the Lemhi Shoshone intermarried with other Shoshone and with Bannock, there was a clear-cut geographical separation between them and the above groups. Some Shoshone wintered in Montana on the other side of the Divide, but they were generally considered to be of the Lemhi band. To the west was the Sawtooth Range and the Tukurika. Although the Tukurika had some contact with the Lemhi people, there were considerable cultural differences between them, owing to the proximity of Plains Indian tribes to the Agaidika and to the different subsistent cycles of the two groups. North of the Lemhi country was the land of the Flathead; to the south the arid Snake River plains intervened between them and the Fort Hall plains population. The Lemhi Shoshone were by no means isolated, but there was considerably less overlapping of activities than in southeastern Idaho.

Winter was usually spent in the valley of the Lemhi River in the area between the modern town of Salmon and the old Mormon post of Fort Lemhi. One informant said that the population was distributed in villages of about a dozen buffalo-hide tipis, each village having a leader. During the winter the population subsisted upon dried stores of berries, roots, and the meat of buffalo and other game. The Lemhi Valley was secure from enemy attack in the winter, for the Blackfoot concentrated their attention on the Bannock encampments on the Snake River.

Other Shoshone were said to have wintered occasionally on the Beaverhead River in Montana. Steward notes that "possibly a few families lived in the vicinity of Dillon, Montana" (1938, p. 188). He lists a large winter camp of some forty families named "Unauvump," which was situated along Red Rock Creek from Lima, Montana, to Red Rock Lake (ibid.). Steward notes that this name refers to the "locomotive" and thus to the Union Pacific Railroad, which follows the Beaverhead River. We obtained the same name, but our informant thought it was merely a place name and not a camp site. Also the site was a short distance up the Beaverhead River from Dillon, Montana. In any case, the reference to the locomotive established the recency of the name. In view of the Blackfoot incursions in that area it is doubtful whether the camp on Red Rock Creek much pre-dated the treaty. However, Bannock and Shoshone buffalo-hunting parties were frequently forced to spend the winter in Montana, although the exact location of these camps is not known.

When winter ended, the Lemhi population did not move far afield in search of subsistence, but hunted and awaited the spring salmon run in April. The Indians fished with harpoons, set basketry traps, and made fish weirs. Most fishing was done in the Lemhi River, but some families fished in the Pahsimeroi River, an affluent of the Salmon River which flowed west of and parallel to the Lemhi. Some fishing took place on the main stream of the Salmon River below its confluence with the Lemhi, but only harpooning was effective owing to the depth of the water.

The weirs were put in the water each spring and dismantled in the fall and stored. Certain men were considered especially proficient in the construction and operation of fish weirs and assumed supervision over the operation.

When the salmon runs had ended, many of the Lemhi people went to Camas Prairie. Some preferred to dig roots in the Lemhi country or to hunt deer in the ranges on either side of the valley. These hunting groups were quite small and usually numbered only two to four tipis. The sojourn on Camas Prairie lasted only about a month and the Lemhi people returned for the summer-fall salmon run. When this was over at the end of August, preparations were made for the trip to the buffalo country.

At least three horses were required for the buffalo hunt: one for the hunter, another for his wife, and a third for packing purposes. Even this number was inadequate, since children also needed mounts and one pack horse was not enough to transport a good take of meat and hides.

Also, the hunter should preferably have a specially trained buffalo horse, which he would ride only while the buffalo herd was being chased. While the Lemhi were richer in horses than were most Shoshone, some people were forced to stay at home. These hunted game in the mountains of the Lemhi region and adjoining areas on the Montana side of the Divide and depended to some extent on the largesse of the returning buffalo party.

The buffalo hunters crossed the Divide through Lemhi Pass to the Beaverhead River and went out to the hunting grounds along the previously described routes. Our informants had no recollection of alliances with other Shoshone or with other tribes on the buffalo hunt except for one who said that the Lemhi Shoshone hunted with Nez Percé parties after an earlier period of hostility. At this earlier time the Nez Percé and the Flathead were said to have been enemies of the Lemhi people. Lemhi informants claimed that the buffalo parties usually succeeded in reaching winter quarters on the Lemhi River before the snows closed the passes. In view of Lewis and Clark's information and our data from Fort Hall, however, it might be supposed that they were often forced to remain in Montana for the winter.

IV. ECOLOGY AND SOCIAL SYSTEM

Out of the mass of detailed data presented in the preceding chapters, certain constant features in the life of the buffalo-hunting Shoshone and Bannock may be discerned. First, there is no doubt of the importance of buffalo in the economy of these people. During an early period, when the Shoshone were among the first tribes of the Northern Plains to adopt the horse, they occupied large areas of the Missouri drainage and extensive buffalo herds were also to be found west of the Continental Divide. Even after tribal pressures from the north forced the Shoshone into residence west of the Rockies part of the time, advantage was still taken of the buffalo in that region. And regular sorties were made over the mountains in search of the more abundant herds there. But no sector of the mounted Shoshone population, at least after 1800, was completely dependent upon the buffalo nor were their principal social connections with the east. Rather, their firmest social ties were with their colinguists to the west, and their economy also was strongly oriented in that direction.

This fact has been a major source of difficulty in our attempt to isolate social groupings among the Bannock and Shoshone. The Bannock, usually accompanied by many Idaho Shoshone, ranged east to central Montana, or into the Big Horn Basin, with the Eastern Shoshone. Part of the year, however, saw them in western Idaho and in Oregon, where they visited and intermarried with the Northern Paiute. Although we have no information on persons shifting membership from the Bannock to the Northern Paiute, such relocations no doubt took place, even if only temporarily. There are ample data, however, to document the reverse process, for Northern Paiute were continually joining the Bannock in order to take part in buffalo hunting.

The same fluidity of movement of individuals and families may be noted among the mounted Shoshone of Idaho, Utah, and Wyoming. Those buffalo hunters whom we have somewhat arbitrarily assigned to Idaho customarily wintered on the Portneuf and upper Snake rivers. But they could be found in different seasons and during various years in northern Utah, on the waters of the Bear River and east of Great Salt Lake, and in western Wyoming. Families occasionally went to the Goose Creek Mountains in the fall for pine nuts, and almost all went down the Snake River in spring and early summer to take part in salmon fishing. In all these places they interacted with and could trace kinship bilaterally to the unmounted, more permanent inhabitants.

This is true also for the so-called Eastern Shoshone. We have shown that these mounted people wintered on the Bear and Green rivers until their final establishment on the Wind River Reservation; in fact, the first Eastern Shoshone Agency was at Fort Bridger. Annual trips were made to Salt Lake City, after its settlement by the Mormons, and visits into Idaho were frequent. Moreover, Shoshone not generally associated with Washakie's leadership who possessed horses joined the latter for buffalo hunting. Evidence for this is most clear in the case of Pocatello's followers. This particular band, found at various times buffalo hunting in central Wyoming, wintering in northern Utah or southeastern Idaho, and fishing or raiding on the Snake River, is an excellent example of the social continuity between Plains and Basin-Plateau. That there was such social continuity, merging, and interpenetration indicates a common set of social understandings, of great similarity in social structure. It may be further argued that this continuity and exchange of population served in some degree to preserve a more amorphous Basin-type society among the buffalo hunters.

It is clear that larger political units existed among the mounted Shoshone and Bannock than among their fellows to the east. We believe, however, that it would be erroneous to attribute great stability or cohesiveness to these aggregates, for the seasonal amalgamation and splitting of other Plains populations is even more pronounced among the Shoshone. The reason for this is partly the fact that the Shoshone spent long periods of the year west of the Rockies and within the range itself. Buffalo hunting did unite most of the mounted people every fall and to a lesser extent in the spring. There is considerable variation of evidence on whether the people crossing the Divide from Wyoming and Idaho formed two large parties or several smaller ones. It may be surmised that the large parties were common in earlier times owing to the threat of enemies, but the smaller ones seem to have been more common later in the nineteenth century, especially after the establishment of the Wind River Reservation. The time spent in the buffalo hunt was closely correlated with the distance to the herds. Our fragmentary accounts suggest that in the upper Green and Snake rivers before 1840, smaller groups hunted for shorter periods. The Big Horn Basin, however, is more than 200 miles from the Green River area, and the bands were forced to travel longer distances and to kill their winter meat supply in one prolonged hunt. Although the Wyoming Shoshone usually were able to return for the winter to the Green and Bear rivers, this was not true of those Idaho Shoshone and Bannock who sought buffalo in Montana. The distance from Camas Prairie in Idaho to the buffalo country of Montana was almost 500 miles, making a winter return to Idaho most difficult and aggravating the problem of packing meat. Many of the Idaho people chose not to make this long and difficult journey and found adequate fall hunting in the local mountains. A buffalo party could thus be on the move for a few days or a week, for two months or seven months, depending on the itinerary followed. Cohesion was closest during actual traveling and hunting. Winter camps were not tightly nucleated settlements of an entire buffalo party, for hunting during the winter required some dispersal. This point deserves some elaboration. Shimkin has stressed the inadequacy of buffalo hunting for a complete winter subsistence (Shimkin, 1947a, p. 266) and this is borne out by the testimony of our informants also. Buffalo meat no doubt supplied the margin of survival, but considerable dependence was placed on elk, deer, moose, rabbits, and other animals during the winter. A very large and compact winter camp would soon exhaust the game in its immediate vicinity. Moreover, the winter location had to be in places where these animals could be found. Camps were thus generally [not] located in river valleys, where wood, water, and protection from storms could be found, but in the vicinity of the high mountains inhabited by the game.

Large population concentrations broke down completely during the summer. Buffalo hunting was restricted to strays and to the small timber buffalo. But the principal game was taken in the mountain country west of the Continental Divide. Large camp groups could not be adapted to the scattered resources used during this period, and people gathered mainly for reasons of defense. Summer groupings of a minimum size seem to have been positively preferred by the Shoshone, as our data from the post-reservation period indicate.

This ecological adaptation and mode of social interaction with other groups had a profound effect on the structure of Shoshone society. Shimkin analyzes the fluctuations in economy and local grouping among the Wind River Shoshone and states (1947a, p. 280):

> It also strengthened the cross-currents of individualism and collective discipline: individual prestige in war honors and hunting versus united military societies and collective bison hunts.

But the basic structure of Shoshone society remained diffuse and atomistic. Institutions productive of centralization were weak. Lowie, for example, reports on police, or soldier, societies among the Eastern Shoshone (Lowie, 1915, pp. 813-814). There were two such groups, called the Yellow Noses and the Logs. The former used inverted speech and were expected to be more courageous. They accordingly were responsible for leading the band when on the march, while the Logs formed the rear guard. Each of these groups had a headman, but Lowie states that the tribal chief was a member of neither. Membership was attained through the candidate's own initiative or by invitation; purchase and age-grading were not criteria, and societies using such means of recruitment were evidently absent among the Eastern Shoshone. Although Lowie did not report the functions of the police societies in detail, he says that the Yellow Nose society, in addition to its responsibility of protecting the traveling bands and maintaining order among them, also policed the hunt. Lowie further writes that the horse of a deviant hunter would be beaten and that any buffalo hides taken by him would be destroyed.

Lowie's information on the Idaho is more fragmentary. We learn only that among the Lemhi Shoshone: "At a dance of hunt, he [the chief] was assisted by di'rakōńe policemen, armed with quirts" (Lowie, 1909, p. 208). Regarding the Lemhi, one of Steward's informants told him that the police institution had been recently introduced (Steward, 1938, p. 194). Steward's data on the police in Idaho is more complete (ibid., p. 211):

> The institution of police, which was obviously borrowed from Wyoming, is of unknown antiquity. It was largely civil and consisted of four or five middle-aged men, Bannock or Shoshoni, who had a civic spirit. They were selected and instructed by the council.

Actual soldier societies were not present in Idaho. The policemen were primarily responsible for keeping the traveling band together and were secondarily concerned with the buffalo hunt.

We specifically queried our Shoshone and Bannock informants on the presence of police societies or of any techniques for control of impulsive buffalo hunters. The responses were all negative, nor is there any historical reference to police societies. The Shoshone and Bannock, we learned from contemporary Indians, needed no coercion to keep them from premature and individual preying upon a buffalo herd. Such action would not be to any individual's self-interest, it was said, and the censure of the community imposed sufficient control over individual behavior. But we cannot deny the existence of the two societies or of the dances associated with them. Rather, we would surmise that the police societies were not important elements in social control nor were they ever a key element in Shoshone social structure; the fact that they have been only imperfectly preserved in traditional knowledge is, itself, of some significance. We hypothesize, then, that the symbolic content of soldier societies had reached the Shoshone without major effects on the ordering of personal and group relations. These conclusions are much akin to Wallace and Hoebel's for the Comanche, who were, it seems, able to hunt buffalo quite effectively without institutionalized coercive restraints (Wallace and Hoebel, 1952, pp. 56-57).

Chieftaincy was more highly developed in the eastern sectors of the Shoshone occupancy than among the people farther west. But even among the mounted bands, the authority of the chiefs was limited. Lewis and Clark commented on the essentially egalitarian nature of Shoshone society, and later travelers present evidence leading to the same conclusion. The wealth differentiation characteristic of the later history of other Plains tribes never became a significant factor among the Shoshone. This is no doubt owing in part to their weak military position and the consequent heavy losses of horses to enemy tribes. Moreover, the Shoshone were only marginally involved in the buffalo-hide trade, and large horse herds and extensive polygyny did not have the utility that they did among, for example, the Blackfoot, who employed women as an essential part of the labor force (cf. Lewis, 1942).

The absence of strong tendencies to stratification and the type of ecological adaptation present acted to inhibit the development of strong authority patterns. Leadership over a large population, such as that exerted by Chief Washakie, was necessarily temporary in nature and was largely restricted to periods when people united for the common enterprises of war and buffalo hunting. During the summer and most of winter and spring a host of minor chiefs of varying influence and prestige were responsible for directing the activities of clusters of followers. Even war and the spring and fall hunts did not necessarily entail the participation of an entire tribe. The buffalo hunters frequently split into smaller hunting parties when out on the plains. And warfare, if offensive, usually was carried on by small raiding parties. Even in defensive warfare attacks were swift and without warning, and large numbers of people could not be gathered to repel the invaders.

"Tribal" chiefs did exist in Idaho and Wyoming, but they exercised discontinuous influence on a group of followers, who might only infrequently all gather as a unit. And since it is impossible to isolate Shoshone or Bannock tribes as stable membership units, the great chiefs may be more profitably viewed as the men of highest prestige within a certain area. The positions of these leaders became more clearly defined in later times, when first traders and then government agents sought them out as representatives of their people. That the white man's image of the chieftaincy was erroneous may be seen in the examples cited of disaffection and the subsequent efforts of the agents to shore up the authority of their delegated chiefs.

Chiefs acted in consultation with councils of distinguished men and lesser chiefs, and the familiar Plains role of camp announcer is also present among the Shoshone. The chief in any area achieved his status through general consensus and recognition of his high prestige. Generosity, wisdom, bravery, and skill in hunting were key criteria for the selection of headmen. The position was neither hereditary nor for life. Although it is not possible to speak of a chief being "deposed," many a chief was replaced by a man whose star was in the ascendancy. And it was also possible for two or three men to have almost equivalent claim to the role within the same district. Despite the nonhereditary nature of the office, we sometimes find it shared by brothers, or sometimes one brother succeeded another. Such cases may be explained as the result of general family prestige or of common upbringing and ideals of conduct.

One important limiting factor on the power of chiefs was the mobility of the population. Individuals could and did move to other areas or join other leaders, and the chief who wished to maintain his influence over his followers could not carry out policy greatly opposed to their wishes. The mobility of the population is a function of several important facts. First, the bands were not corporate units in the sense of groups holding rights over strategic resources. As we have seen, there were no such limits within the general range of Shoshone-speaking people. Band territoriality would have been directly contradictory to the enormous distances traversed by the mounted people. The region, as a whole, presented the possibility of a balanced diet and annual subsistence cycle, but smaller subdivisions of it could not do so, though they provided overabundance of a limited number of foods in certain seasons. Even the area of Shoshone occupation, as compared with other peoples' territory, was vague and ill defined. Territory, as such, was not a matter of great concern in the relations of the Shoshone with hostile tribes. Rather, they vigorously defended their horses and their own lives during enemy invasions. The buffalo country east of the mountains was roamed over by several groups, as were the mountain areas of western Wyoming and Montana. And peaceful groups of the Basin-Plateau merged and intermingled with the Shoshone in the areas in which they had contact.

The individual, the family, or the group of families that elected to change leaders within an area or to shift from one area to another did not give up vested rights and prerogatives. And, given the loose nature of Shoshone social structure and the diffuse and widespread network of social relationships, the person or group seeking a change could usually count upon acceptance elsewhere. The reservation system tended to tighten political organization and to define groupings more closely, since reservation membership did constitute a vested interest and government legitimation and stabilization of a central chieftaincy restricted the choices open to the individual.

The principal item in the productive apparatus of the mounted Shoshone was the horse. Without sufficient horses to pursue the buffalo hunt, the Indian was relegated to "digger" status and had to remain within the Great Basin. But horses were individual, private property, and a man could locate under any leadership as long as he was mounted. His primary economic dependency was thus shifted from the larger social group to his own herd. Each man was to a large extent his own master and acted accordingly.

The loose bilaterality of the Shoshone was ideally adapted to their mode of existence. Our data show some tendency toward matrilocality, but Steward states that, in Idaho, this is true primarily of the early years of marriage, after which the couple could exercise a bilocal option (Steward, 1938, p. 214). The direction of the choice depended on such situational factors as the prestige of either mate's parents or their wealth in horses. In any event, there was no marked preferential weighting of either line. Our informants reported that the married couple often shifted back and forth for varying periods of time. Ultimately, the mounted Shoshone may be just as profitably looked on as neolocal, as were the western Shoshone, for the couple did not necessarily live with or adjacent to either mate's parents. People were quite free to join other relatives or to associate closely with unrelated persons. This, and the periodic splitting up and reamalgamation of larger groups, inhibited any development of large, solidary nuclei of bilateral kinsmen. Relationships were traced bilaterally and widely, but ties were amorphous and weak. Lacking bounded and corporate kin groups, persons were highly individuated and possessed maximum geographical mobility.

We may well conclude that, from the point of view of social structure, the mounted Shoshone were typologically much like the Great Basin people with whom they had close relations. Easily diffused items of culture, such as their material inventory, many religious beliefs, and their mode of warfare, establish their intimate historical connection with the Plains. But the higher levels of social integration found among the Shoshone are of a situational nature and are not well integrated with the fundamental facts of family life and more stable modes of grouping. It would be erroneous to conclude from this, however, that this amorphous, Basinlike social structure was nonadaptive to the Plains. That it is not at all atypical of the area is indicated by Eggan's statement (1955, pp. 518-519):

> Plains Indian society, despite its lack of lineage and clan, still has a social structure. This structure is "horizontal" or generational in character and has little depth. The extended family groupings in terms of matrilocal residence or centered around a sibling group are amorphous but flexible. The bilateral or composite band organization, centered around a chief and his close relatives, may change its composition according to various circumstances-economic or political. The camp-circle encompasses the tribe, provides a disciplined organization for the communal hunt, and a center for the Sun Dance and other tribal ceremonies which symbolized the renewed unity of the tribe and the renewal of nature. The seasonal alternation between band and tribal camp-circle is related to ecological changes in the environment, and particularly to the behavior of the buffalo...

> The working hypothesis proposed earlier ... that "tribes coming into the Plains with different backgrounds and social systems," can be tentatively extended to Plains social structure as a whole, despite the variations noted. That this is in large measure an internal adjustment to the uncertain and changing conditions of Plains environment-ecological and social-rather than a result of borrowing and diffusion, is still highly probable.

The loose bilaterality seen by Eggan as a characteristic of Plains society was part of the earlier Shoshone social background. But more centralized political units and predominantly "horizontal" organizations, such as age-grade and soldier societies, were more weakly developed than among many other tribes of the northern Plains. This fact, as well as the acquisition of firearms by the northern tribes, may have been responsible for the manifest military weakness of the Shoshone and their westward retreat beyond the Rocky Mountains.

BIBLIOGRAPHY

Abbreviations

AA	American Anthropologist
AMNH-AP	American Museum of Natural History, Anthropological Papers. New York
BAE-B	Bureau of American Ethnology, Bulletin
CD	Congressional Document, Washington
MPUS	Report of the President of the United States. Washington
RCIA	Report of the Commissioner of Indian Affairs. Washington
RSI	Report of the Secretary of the Interior. Washington
RSW	Report of the Secretary of War. Washington
UC	University of California Publications. Berkeley and Los Angeles
-AAE	American Archaeology and Ethnology
-AR	Anthropological Records

Alter, J. Cecil
1925. James Bridger. Salt Lake City, Utah.
Ballard, D. W.
1867. RCIA 1866, CD 1284, pp. 190-192.
1869. RCIA 1868, CD 1366, pp. 656-659.
Beckwith, Lieut. E. G.
1855. Report of Explorations for a Route for the Pacific Railroad, of the Line of the Forty-First Parallel of North Latitude 1854. CD 792, 1B, 1854-55. Washington.
Beckwourth, James P.
1931. The Life and Adventures of J. P. Beckwourth. T. D. Bonner, ed. New York.
Blythe, Beatrice
1938. "Northern Paiute Bands in Oregon," AA 40:402-405.
Bryant, Edwin
1885. Rocky Mountain Adventures. Hurst and Co., New York.
Burpee, L. J. (ed.)
1927. Journals and Letters of Pierre Gaultier de Varennes de La Vérendrye and His Sons. Toronto.
Burton, Richard F.
1861. The City of the Saints. London.
Campbell, Albert H.
1859. RSI 1859, CD 984, pp. 3-12.
Campbell, J. A.
1870. RCIA 1869, CD 1414, pp. 171-173.
1871. RCIA 1870, CD 1449, pp. 638-642.

Chittenden, Hiram Martin
1933. Yellowstone National Park, Stanford, Calif.
Connelley, William Elsay
1907. Doniphan's Expedition and the Conquest of Mexico and New California. Topeka, Kan.
Cooley, D. N.
1866. RCIA 1865, CD 1248, pp. 169-225.
Coutant, C.
1899. History of Wyoming. Laramie, Wyo.
Crawford, Medorem
1897. Journal of M. Crawford. Sources of the History of Oregon, Vol. 1, No. 1. Eugene, Ore.
Cross, Major Osborne
1851. RSW 1850, CD 587, pp. 128-231.
Dale, Harrison Clifford
1918. The Ashley-Smith Explorations and the Discovery of a Central Route to the Pacific, 1822-1829. Cleveland, Ohio.
Danilson, W. H.
1870. RCIA 1869, CD 1414, pp. 729-730.
De Smet, Pierre Jean
1905. Life, Letters, and Travels of Father Jean De Smet, S.J., 1801-1873. New York.
1906. Letters and Sketches. *In* Early Western Travels, 1748-1846, Vol. 27. R. G. Thwaites, ed. Cleveland, Ohio.
Doty, James Duane
1863. RCIA 1862, CD 1157, pp. 342-344, 354-358.
1865. RCIA 1864, CD 1220, pp. 317-320.
Dunn, J. P.
1886. Massacres of the Mountains. New York.
Eggan, Fred
1955. Social Anthropology: Methods and Results. *In* Social Anthropology of North American Indian Tribes. F. Eggan, ed. (2d ed.). Chicago.
Ewers, John C.
1955. The Horse in Blackfoot Indian Culture. BAE-B 159.
Farnham, Thomas J.
1843. Travels in the Great Western Prairies, the Anahuac and Rocky Mountains, and in the Oregon Territory. New York.
1906. Travels in the Great Western Prairies, the Anahuac and Rocky Mountains, and in the Oregon Territory. *In* Early Western Travels, 1748-1846. Vol. 28. R. G. Thwaites, ed. Cleveland, Ohio.
Ferris, Warren Angus
1940. Life in the Rocky Mountains. Paul C. Phillips, ed. Denver, Colo.
Fleming, G. W.
1871. RCIA 1870, CD 1449, pp. 642-644.
Fleming, H. B.
1858. MPUS 1857, CD 956, p. 167.
Floyd-Jones, De L.
1870. RCIA 1869, CD 1414, pp. 719-721.
1871. RCIA 1870, CD 1449, pp. 645-647.
Forney, Jacob
1859. RCIA 1858, CD 974, pp. 561-565.
1860*a*. RCIA 1859, CD 1023, pp. 730-741.
1860*b*. MPUS 1859, CD 1033, pp. 44-45, 52-53, 59-60, 117-118.
Fremont, John Charles

1845. Report of the Exploring Expedition to the Rocky Mountains in the Year 1842, and to Oregon and North California in the Years 1843-1844.

Fuller, Harrison
1875. RCIA 1874, CD 1639, pp. 572-573.

Gove, Captain Jesse A.
1928. The Utah Expedition, 1857-58. New Hampshire Historical Society Collections, Vol. 12. Otis G. Hammond, ed. Concord, N. H.

Haines, Francis
1938. The Northward Spread of Horses among the Plains Indians, AA 40:429-437.

Hale, Horatio
1848. Hale's Indians of Northwest America and Vocabularies of North America. Transactions of the American Ethnological Society, Vol. 2. New York.

Hamilton, W. T.
1905. My Sixty Years on the Plains. E. T. Sieber, ed. New York.

Head, F. H.
1867. RCIA 1866, CD 1284, pp. 122-126.
1868. RCIA 1867, CD 1326, pp. 173-180, 186-188.
1869. RCIA 1868, CD 1366, pp. 608-614.

Hebard, Grace R.
1930. Washakie. Cleveland, Ohio.

Hickman, Bill
1872. Brigham's Destroying Angel. New York.

Hodge, Frederick Webb (ed.)
1910. Handbook of American Indians North of Mexico. BAE-B 30, Pt. 2.

Hoebel, E. Adamson
1938. Bands and Distributions of the Eastern Shoshone. AA 40:410-413.

Holeman, John H.
1852. RCIA 1852, CD 613, pp. 444-446.
1854. RCIA 1853, CD 690, pp. 443-447.
1858. MPUS 1857, CD 956, pp. 139-148, 151-155, 158-161.

Hough, George C.
1867. RCIA 1866, CD 1284.
1869. RCIA 1868, CD 1366, pp. 660-661.

Hultkrantz, A.
1949. Kulturbildningen hos Wyomings Shoshoni-indianer. Ymer, pp. 134-157. Stockholm.
1954. Indianerna i Yellowstone Park. Ymer, h. 2. Stockholm.
1958. Tribal Divisions within the Eastern Shoshoni of Wyoming, Proceedings, 32nd International Congress of Americanists, Copenhagen, pp. 148-154.

Hurt, Garland
1856. RCIA 1855, CD 810, pp. 517-521.

Irish, O. H.
1865. RCIA 1864, CD 1220, pp. 313-315.
1866. RCIA 1865, CD 1248, pp. 310-316.

Irving, Washington
1837. The Rocky Mountains, *In* The Journal of Captain B. L. E. Bonneville. Philadelphia.
1850. Astoria. Covent Garden.
1873. The Adventures of Captain Bonneville, U. S. A. *In* The Rocky Mountains and the Far West. (Knickerbocker ed.). Philadelphia.
[1890.] Astoria. Thomas Y. Crowell and Co., New York.

Irwin, James
1874. RCIA 1873, CD 1601, pp. 612-613.

Jones, Capt. W. A.

1875. Report upon the Reconnaissance of Northwestern Wyoming, chap. I, pp. 5-44. U. S. Engineer Dept., Washington.

Kirkpatrick, J. M.
1863. RCIA 1862, CD 1157, pp. 409-412.

Kroeber, A. L.
1909. The Bannock and Shoshoni Languages, AA 11:266-277.
1939. Cultural and Natural Areas of Native North America. UC-PAAE Vol. 38.

Lander, F. W.
1859. RSI 1859, CD 984, pp. 47-73. 1860. RSW 1859, CD 1033, pp. 121-139.

Lane, Joseph
1851. RCIA 1851, CD 587, pp. 156-168.

Langworthy, Franklin
1932. Scenery of the Plains, Mountains and Mines. Paul C. Phillips, ed. Princeton, N. J.

Leonard, Zenas
1934. Narrative of the Adventures of Zenas Leonard. Milo M. Quaife, ed. Chicago.

Lewis, Meriwether, and William Clark 1904-06. Original Journals of the Lewis and Clark Expedition, 1804-06. 8 vols. R. G. Thwaites, ed. New York.

Lewis, Oscar
1942. The Effects of White Contact upon Blackfoot Culture, with Special Reference to the Role of the Fur Trade. American Ethnological Society, Philadelphia. 73 pp.

Lowie, Robert H.
1909. The Northern Shoshone. AMNH-AP 2:169-306.
1915. Dances and Societies of the Shoshone Indians. AMNH-AP 11 (pt. 10):803-835.

Lyon, Caleb
1866. RCIA 1865, CD 1248, pp. 415-419.
1867. RCIA 1866, CD 1284, p. 187.

Mann, Luther
1865. RCIA 1865, CD 1248, pp. 326-328.
1868. RCIA 1867, CD 1326, pp. 182-184, 189.
1869. RCIA 1868, CD 1366, pp. 616-619.
1870. RCIA 1869, CD 1414, pp. 715-716.

Margry, P. (ed.)
1888. Journal du voyage fait par le Chevalier de la Vérendrye. *In* Découvertes et établissements des Francais dans l'Ouest et dans le Sud de l'Amerique Septentrionale, 1614-1754, 6:598-601.

Mullan, Lieut. John
1855. RSW 1854, CD 758, pp. 322-349.

Ogden, Peter Skene
1909. Journals of the Snake Expeditions, 1825-1826. T. C. Elliott, ed. Oregon Historical Quarterly, 10 (no. 4):331-365.
1910. Journals of the Snake Expeditions, 1826-1827. T. C. Elliott, ed. Oregon Historical Quarterly, 11 (no. 2):201-222.
1950. Peter Skene Ogden's Snake Country Journals, 1824-1825 and 1825-1826. E. E. Rich, ed. The Hudson's Bay Record Society, Vol. 13. London.

Patten, James I.
1878. RCIA 1877, CD 1800, pp. 603-606.

Patterson, J. H.
1870. RCIA 1869, CD 1414, pp. 717-718.

Powell, Chas. F.
1868. RCIA 1867, CD 1326, pp. 251-253.
1869. RCIA 1868, CD 1366, pp. 661-663.
1870. RCIA 1869, CD 1414, pp. 728-729.

Powell, J. W., and G. W. Ingalls
1874. RCIA 1873, CD 1601, pp. 409-442.
Rainsford, J. C.
1873. RCIA 1872, CD 1560, pp. 666-667.
Raynolds, W. F.
1868. RSW 1867, CD 1317, pp. 1-174.
Remy, Jules, and Julius Brenchley
1861. A Journey to Great Salt Lake City. Vol. 1. London.
Ross, Alexander
1924. The Fur Hunters of the Far West. Milo M. Quaife, ed. Chicago.
Russell, Osborne
1921. Journal of a Trapper, or Nine Years in the Rocky Mountains, 1834-1843. Boise, Idaho.
1955. Journals of a Trapper. Aubrey L. Haines, ed. Oregon Historical Society.
Schoolcraft, H. R.
1860. Archives of Aboriginal Knowledge. Vol. I. Philadelphia.
Shanks, John P. C., T. W. Bennett, and Henry W. Reed
1874. RSI 1873, CD 1608, pp. 2-4.
Shaw, Reuben C.
1948. Across the Plains in Forty-nine. M. M. Quaife, ed. Chicago.
Shimkin, D. B.
1938. "Wind River Shoshone Geography," AA 40:413-415. 1939. Shoshone-Comanche Origins and Migrations. Proceedings, Sixth Pacific Science Congress, 4:17-25.
1947*a*. Wind River Shoshone Ethnogeography. UC-AR 5:245-288.
1947*b*. Childhood and Development among the Wind River Shoshone. UC-AR 5:289-325.
Simpson, George
1931. Fur Trade and Empire. Frederick Merk, ed. Cambridge, Mass.
Stansbury, Howard
1852. Exploration and Survey of the Valley of the Great Salt Lake of Utah. Sen. Ex. Doc. No. 3, spec. sess., March, 1851. Philadelphia.
Steward, Julian H.
1937. Linguistic Distributions and Political Groups of the Great Basin Shoshoneans, AA 39:625-634. 1938. Basin-Plateau Aboriginal Sociopolitical Groups. BAE-B 120.
1939. Some Observations on Shoshonean Distributions, AA 41:261-265.
Stewart, Omer C.
1939. The Northern Paiute Bands. UC-AR 2:127-149.
Stuart, Robert
1935. The Discovery of the Oregon Trail; Robert Stuart's Narrative of the Overland Trip Eastward from Astoria in 1812-13. New York.
Sully, Alf.
1870. RCIA 1869, CD 1414, pp. 731-735.
Talbot, Theodore
1931. The Journals of Theodore Talbot, 1843 and 1849-52. Charles H. Carey, ed. Portland, Ore.
Taylor, N. G.
1869. RCIA 1868, CD 1366, pp. 683-684.
Thompson, R. R.
1855. RCIA 1854, CD 746, pp. 489-493.
Townsend, John K.
1905. Narrative of a Journey across the Rocky Mountains ... 1834. *In* Early Western Travels, 1748-1846. Vol. XXI. R. G. Thwaites, ed. Cleveland, Ohio.
Tyrell, J. B. (ed.)

1916. David Thompson's Narrative of His Explorations in Western North America, 1784-1812. Publications of the Champlain Society, Vol. 12. Toronto.

Viall, J. A.
1872. RCIA 1871, CD 1505, pp. 825-833.

Wagner, Will. H.
1861. Letter from the Acting Secretary of the Interior,
1860-61, CD 1100, pp. 20-26.

Wallace, Ernest, and E. Adamson Hoebel
1952. The Comanches: Lords of the South Plains. Norman, Okla.

Wallen, H. D.
1859. Affairs in Oregon, CD 1051. Washington.

War of the Rebellion
1902. Series I, Vol. 50. Government Printing Office. Washington.

Wheeler, George M.
1875. Preliminary Report upon a Reconnaissance through Southern and Southeastern Nevada, 1869. U. S. Army Engineering Dept.

Wilkes, Charles (U.S.N.)
1845. Narrative of the United States Exploring Expedition during the Years 1838, 1839, 1840, 1841, 1842. Vol. 4. Philadelphia.

Wilson, E. N.
1926. The White Indian Boy. Yonkers-on-Hudson, N.Y.

Wilson, John
1849. RCIA 1849, CD 570, pp. 1002-1004.

Wislizenus, F. A.
1912. A Journey to the Rocky Mountains in the Year 1839. St. Louis, Mo.

Wissler, Clark
1910. Material Culture of the Blackfoot Indians. AMNH-AP 5 (pt. 1):1-175.
1920. North American Indians of the Plains. New York.

Work, John
1923. The Journal of John Work. Cleveland, Ohio.
1945. Fur Brigade to the Bonaventura. Alice B. Mahoney, ed. San Francisco.

Wyeth, Nathaniel J.
1899. The Correspondence and Journals of Captain Nathaniel J. Wyeth. *In* Sources of the History of Oregon, Vol. 1, pts. 3-6. Eugene, Ore.

Young, Brigham
1852. RCIA 1852, CD 658, pp. 437-439.
1858. RCIA 1857, CD 919, pp. 598-600.